# SECOND STAR TO THE RIGHT
## AND OTHER SMALL BITES STORIES

INDIES UNITED PUBLISHING HOUSE, LLC
P.O. BOX 3071
QUINCY, IL 62305-3071

www.indiesunited.net

*Dedicated to every person who ever took a chance on an unknown author.*
*Thank you.*

# Table of Contents

# SECOND STAR TO THE RIGHT

## AND OTHER SMALL BITES STORIES

AN
INDIES UNITED PUBLISHING HOUSE
MULTI-AUTHOR ANTHOLOGY

Small Bites
Grand Prize
Winner
2024
Indies United
Publishing House

# Second Star to the Right

• ● ⬤ ● •

## D. Krauss

## Urban Fantasy

Someone knocked on Talbert's back door, which was a bit surprising but he was a man long lived and accustomed to the world so he opened the door with a curious caution and there stood a black child, maybe 12, 13 years old, a boy, nicely dressed and looking at him expectantly. "Yes?" Talbert asked.

"Mister, can I play in your backyard?"

A bit startling, that, and, despite his natural aplomb, Talbert blinked at the child. "What's wrong with your own backyard?"

"I don't have one."

Talbert took a long significant look over the child's

shoulder at the yard next door visible through the half fence. "It looks like it's still there."

The child furrowed a brow then followed Talbert's gaze. "That's not mine."

"You're not related to Mrs. Jackson?"

Shake of the head.

The Jackson's were black so he had assumed ... you know what happens when you do that. Hmm. Okay. "Why my backyard?"

The kid raised shoulders. "It's nice."

"Yes, and I'd like for it remain that way. Will you be careful?"

The boy nodded eagerly.

Talbert splayed hands. "Okay, sure." And the boy shouted, "Thanks mister!" and raced down the deck and off the back steps and Talbert wondered at himself. Are you becoming even more addled, old boy? You let some strange kid commandeer your very meticulously maintained backyard? Best rethink this.

But he didn't want to come off as That Guy, the old fart at the end of the street yelling "Get off my lawn!" at all the kids passing by. So, he pulled a couple of sodas out of the fridge and went to see how much damage the kid had already inflicted.

The kid was inflicting no damage. In fact, he was doing nothing but standing in the middle of the patch of grass between the vegetable garden and the patio, hands jammed into his pockets, big grin on his face, staring upward through the beech tree limbs.

"What are you doing?" Talbert asked.

"Nuthin'."

Talbert laughed at that standard kid response. "Here," Talbert said and handed him a can and the boy smiled even broader, if that was possible, and said, "Thanks, Mister!" and took a big swig.

"So what were you playing?" Talbert asked, after his own big swig.

"Nuthin'."

"Hmm." Talbert set the can down on a deck railing. "No fun playing by yourself, is it?"

The boy shrugged and looked off.

"Do you have anyone else to play with?"

A shrug.

"No other friends?"

Repeat.

The tragedy of these times, Talbert knew. No one had kids anymore, and the ones who did kept them inside, fearful of a world more dangerous by reputation than actuality.

"Well, that sucks." Talbert supposed he could be a substitute, although his gout was acting up. "What would you like to play?"

Another shrug.

"Sports?"

"Yeah!" The boy was immediately enthusiastic.

Great. There goes my gout, Talbert thought. "Well,"

Talbert said, "I am not in the best of shape but there is a basketball hoop at the cul de sac at the end of the street. Do you have a basketball?"

Shake of the head.

"Neither do I." Talbert thought a minute more and had a bright idea. "Okay, there's a young man named Carson who lives next door. He is away at college but I'll bet his mother, Mrs. Jackson, will let you play with one of his basketballs. Just tell her that I sent you over and if there's a question, come get me. I will meet you at the hoop." The boy grinned broadly and ran back up the deck and out the yard and Talbert congratulated himself on the very diplomatic way he had saved his backyard and, ya know, throwing the ball at a hoop just might be the thing on a cool summer morning. So Talbert went in and, after a bit of a search, located his Pumas and sweats and walked out the front door and down to the old basketball hoop that had been Carson's, or more accurately, Carson's dad's, who had left it there as a neighborhood asset. The backboard was broken here and there and the net had long ago disappeared but it was still serviceable.

The boy was standing underneath it clutching a worn basketball. "She said I have to bring it back when we're done."

"As is appropriate. Horse?"

"What?"

"The game, Horse. You've never heard of it?"

Shake of the head. "Okay. It's simple and fun. You take your shot and if you sink the basket, I have to sink one from the same location and style or I earn a letter. The first person to spell out 'horse' loses. Understand?"

The boy nodded eagerly. "You start," Talbert said and the boy reared back and hurled the ball as hard as he could and Talbert watched it ricochet, ending up underneath Anne-across-the-street's Nissan. Talbert looked at the boy. "Have you never shot a basketball before?"

"No."

Talbert was somewhat surprised, but then remembered his earlier stereotyping of the child and maybe he shouldn't presume that the kid knew basketball. Maybe didn't have a Dad, and here you are stereotyping again, you old white man.

"Ah, uhm hm," Talbert cleared his throat. "Alright. Go retrieve the ball — I'm a little too old to be reaching under cars — and I'll show you how."

The boy ran off and came back with the ball in his arms and stood before Talbert. Make no further assumptions, shall we, Talbert old boy? "Let's see you dribble it," he commanded.

"What?"

"Dribble the ball."

"What's that?"

Talbert cocked his head. "You've never played basketball nor ever heard of it, have you?"

The boy hung his head. Talbert, check your assumptions. "It's okay. Everyone has to start somewhere. The object of the game is to toss the ball through the top of the hoop, called the net because there's usually one hanging off the bottom which gives a rather satisfying 'swish' sound when the ball goes through" – here the boy giggled – "and earning two points. You play two halves, usually thirty minutes each but I think they're shorter now, two quarters per half with a halftime of ten minutes in between. The winner is the one with the most points at the end of the second half. You have to pass the ball or dribble it to go forward. To dribble, you bounce it off the floor and back up to your hand. Let me see you do that."

The boy slapped the ball hard against the asphalt, almost getting a face full of leather for his trouble. "No, no." Talbert took the ball. "Control it with your fingers, not your palm. Like this," and Talbert did a passable dribble, eventually bringing it close to the ground and speeding up. He smiled to himself: still got it. "Here." After a bit, the boy had a decent dribble and Talbert nodded. "Okay, so this is how you shoot," and Talbert stood back, aimed the ball and pushed with his back hand. The ball bounced on the rim and went through, to an accompanying "Whoa!" by the boy. Yep, still got it. "Now, you try."

After about thirty minutes, the boy could do a serviceable forward and backward dribble, pass, and shoot. He learned the backboard was his friend and was getting about half of his baskets. "Pretty good for someone who hasn't played before," Talbert said. "Now, you ready for Horse?"

The boy lost, but was game throughout, and Talbert used the opportunity to show him the layup and the outside shot. The boy caught on and did a respectable job. And laughed at the end and said, "That was fun, but I gotta go home now," and Talbert looked up and was surprised how late it was. Time flies. "All right. I'll return the ball. You can head out."

The boy smiled. "Thanks, mister," and hoofed up the street to the main road and was gone.

"Who was that?" Carson's Mom asked when Talbert knocked on her door.

"No idea." He handed the ball over. "Don't even know his name."

"Huh. Well, nice of you to play with him."

"It's not like I'm doing anything else," he said wryly and she laughed and said, "Anytime you want the ball, let me know. Carson will be happy it's being used."

"How is he, by the way?"

"Oh, you know." And there ensued a ten-minute conversation about kids becoming young men and college antics and Talbert walked away amused and went into his house and mused how young becomes old, and old fades away. He made a spaghetti dinner and watched TV and went to bed.

In the morning, someone knocked on his back door and he opened it and the same child stood there, but with four other boys. "Hello," Talbert said, "who's this?"

"These are my friends," the boy waved a hand to include them, one Latino, one Asian, and two other black kids. "Do you want to play with us?"

Thought you didn't have any friends, kid, and had the distinct feeling of being bamboozled, but it was a fun little fraud so, "Sure. Let me finish my coffee first. Why don't you go next door and grab the ball and I'll meet you at the hoop?" And the boys raced off, chirping and excited, and Talbert shook his head, amused. Getting up first thing in the morning and heading outside to play with your friends … "I'm a kid again," he chuckled to himself and downed the coffee and put on his shoes and went down the street.

The other four boys didn't know how to play, either, but, between Talbert and the first boy, they got them into reasonable basketball shape after a half hour or so and they played Horse, with the Latino kid winning to great acclaim from the others, and then they played a five-on-one actual game, with Talbert the one and he was trounced and wheezing and happier than he had been in the longest time.

"Whew," he said, "you guys are killing me." He sat on the curb and drew big breaths and waved at the ER nurse, what's his name, Riley? yeah, that's it, who lived down the street and who was standing on his lawn watching with a big smile on his face. "Y'all thirsty?"

"Nah," the first boy said.

"How 'bout some lunch, then?" Talbert offered. "I make pretty good cheese sandwiches."

"Nah," the Asian boy said, "we're not hungry."

"Really? After all that?" Talbert cocked his head in curiosity. "At your age, I was always starving."

The boys all smiled but said nothing and Talbert figured they were all too polite to ask for food from someone they didn't know. Let's fix that. "I'm Talbert, by the way."

"We know," the first boy said, tossing the ball up and down, up and down.

"You know? Okay, well, what's your name?"

"We gotta go," said suddenly and the ball was bouncing on the street where it was dropped and the five boys went racing towards the corner, laughing and calling and pushing each other and Talbert felt a surge in his heart and was halfway to his feet to join them, just join them.

"Hey, you've got a team now, huh?" Riley joked as Talbert came opposite, dribbling the ball along.

"I suppose so. Have you ever seen them before?"

"Those kids? No, never." Riley furrowed a brow. "Aren't they with you?"

"No. Never saw 'em until yesterday."

"Hmm," Riley considered. "Well, they've certainly latched on to you."

"I suppose. You think maybe they're from that orphanage across town?"

Riley smiled. "I think they call it a 'home' now."

"Yeah, yeah." Talbert waved that away. "Your generation and its word butchery. But do you think they are?"

Riley shrugged. "Maybe. Kind of a distance, though."

"True." Talbert considered. "But we used to think nothing about walking a couple of miles to play with friends."

Riley laughed, "Your generation and your staying out all day thing."

Talbert conceded the point and brought the ball back and considered that, yes, kids didn't play outside anymore because, Riley, your generation thinks video games are the same thing and no wonder no one knows how to shoot a basketball. A shame. It's much more fun actually going out and doing things. Talbert leaned back and savored the morning.

"Hope you come back," Talbert said to the air and went inside to make a grilled cheese.

The next morning, Talbert was in the front yard trimming hedges when the first boy walked up to the gate and said, "Hey, Mr. Talbert!"

Talbert looked up and smiled and said, "Just Talbert and ..." his voice trailed as the four other boys from yesterday gathered around the first one, an additional five or six other boys of various shapes and races forming up behind them, all smiling, all expectant. "My goodness!" Talbert said. "You've got a regular army now!"

The boys all laughed and pushed at each other and looked at Talbert with shining eyes and just at that moment the sun came out from behind a cloud and shone bright and wonderful and a breeze picked up, smelling of honeysuckle and hot asphalt and, wow, it was like a summer day when he was ten. Talbert rocked back and took in a lungful and he'd not had this good of a feeling in such a long time. He smiled at the kids. Young people make you feel young.

"So it looks like we've got two teams here," Talbert glanced over the boys. "Want me to go get Carson's ball and meet me down at the hoop?"

The first boy shook his head and said, "No, we want to play a different game." And he held up a football.

"Ah!" Talbert laughed. "Excellent!" A thought occurred to him. "Do you know how to play?"

To a boy, they all shook their heads.

"Wouldn't you know," Talbert said more to himself than them. "Okay, well, we need a field for that and the closest one is a bit far so let me change out of these boots and …" he stopped talking. The boys had all turned and were looking towards the construction lot next to the railroad tracks back behind the neighborhood and Talbert was going to say no, private property and kind of dangerous but, wait, wait … what is that? Some kind of pathway, trees lining it almost like a tunnel and Talbert could see an open area, rich and lush with grass beyond and, what? Twenty years he had been here, and never noticed it.

"What's going on?" he whispered.

But the boys all whooped and jumped and grabbed at each other and were a boy scrum racing across the cul de sac and past the sagging construction fences and up the tree tunnel. "Wait!" Talbert called, "I gotta get my shoes!" And they laughed and waved him to come on, come on! And Talbert spun about and went into the house and a frantic search and he had his sneakers pulled on and he hesitated because he should lock up and check things and no, the boys are calling and he was out the front door and cleared the steps without touching one and he was running like he had not run in years.

Decades.

He got there and showed them how to pass, how to take a three-point stance and soft tackle because they didn't have pads but, hey, boys are going to get hurt so walk it off and rub some dirt on it and they played and ran and scored and knocked each other down and the last time Talbert got up from the bottom of the pile he no longer towered over them, was no longer wheezing, was looking everyone in the eye, everyone laughing and singing and happy and ten years old and Talbert was, too.

"Who are you?" Talbert asked in his boy voice. "What are you?"

They all smiled and looked up from hands on knees and there were hills off to the side, golden, grass covered, and the boys headed for them and Talbert followed.

2nd
Place
Small Bites
Short Story Contest
2024
Indies United
Publishing House

# The Manikin

## Donald Firesmith

## Science Fiction

Three other medical students and I were waiting in a meeting room just down the hall from the operating room, where we would take our fifth and final exam to determine whether we were ready to graduate and start our residency working on actual patients. Emberly was our budding anesthesiologist, while Ellie and Dominic would be our two surgical nurses. And then there was me, Milo Mackensie. I would be the surgeon.

We had all passed the previous four exams, during which we treated a broken arm, a mysterious infection, a laparoscopic appendectomy, and a bowel resection. This final exam would test our skills in treating a patient with a life-threatening injury. As before, our professors would only provide basic information about the test scenario prior to the beginning of the exam.

"So, what do you think it will be?" Dominic asked. "My bet is it involves a patient who was in a car wreck. They're common and certainly something we'll encounter in real life."

"I'm thinking maybe someone with multiple gunshot wounds," Emberly replied. "If we're in a big city trauma center, shootings would be a daily occurrence. How about you, Milo? What do you think it might be?"

"I honestly have no idea," I replied. "Since this is the final exam, it's bound to be something extremely serious. Something bad enough that we could lose the patient if we're not careful. How about you, Ellie? What do you think?"

Before she could answer, the door opened, and our three professors, who would oversee our exam, walked in. Dr. Reinholt, who was a highly experienced general surgeon, would grade my performance. Dr. Isaacson, who taught anesthesiology, would give Emberly her score. Finally, Professor Lemont would grade Ellie's and Dominic's performance.

Professor Reinholt explained the exam's scenario. "For today's exam, we will simulate working in a major trauma center. A mass shooting at a local middle school has resulted in multiple deaths. Dozens of adults and children with one or more gunshot wounds are arriving in the ER. The shooter used an assault-style rifle. As you learned in your first-year class, these weapons fire high-velocity, low-mass bullets that tumble on impact and rapidly deposit their kinetic energy into the surrounding flesh and bones. Expect your patient to present with small entry wounds, large exit wounds, and massive internal tissue damage and destruction."

I couldn't help remembering the videos and images of the horrible injuries we had seen in class. Worse was the memory of observing an autopsy of a young man killed by such a weapon of war. It is no wonder the vast majority of the medical community opposed assault weapons and wanted them banned.

"Your goal today is to save your patient's life," Professor Reinholt continued. "Due to the scenario's high number of casualties, assume that other patients will require your attention and access to your trauma bay as soon as you have finished with this one. Prioritize your work, focus on the most critical injuries, and stabilize the patient for transfer to a regular operating room for further surgery. We will assess not only on the quality of the medical care you provide but also on the speed with which you work."

Dr. Isaacson provided further details about the exam. "Because of the large number of casualties arriving simultaneously, the test scenario has the four of you working completely on your own during this exam. We will not interfere or be available to answer questions until after the exam. Your other professors and I will observe your live video feeds from the cameras in the trauma bay. And please remember that in addition to grading you on your individual work, we will also assess your ability to work effectively as a team."

Professor Lemont gave us our final instructions before the exam. "We've recently received a shipment of manikins with the latest AI upgrade, and you will be the first students to one of them. As before, these lab-grown human bodies are virtually identical to real patients with the exception that they lack the cerebrum with its higher brain functions. According to American Android Corporation's promotion and user guide videos, the new manikins behave more realistically than their previous version. Expect your manikin to have realistic psychological reactions and perfectly simulate how a human would react, both in terms of pain, fear, confusion, and shock and in how they will interact with you. And though the manikin is not conscious and has no subjective awareness, we still expect you to treat it with the same compassion and professionalism afforded to real patients. Are there any final questions before we begin?"

We exchanged glances and shook our heads.

"Okay, for this exam, we set up room three as a trauma bay," Professor Reinholt said. "Put on your PPE and get ready for the arrival of your patient. You have ten minutes to prepare."

We quickly donned the impervious gowns, gloves, goggles, and booties that comprised our personal protective equipment. Once we entered room three, we immediately got to work. Emberly laid out the intubation instruments: a laryngoscope and because she didn't know the size she would need, a variety of endotracheal tubes. After preparing the supplies needed to put in IV lines, Ellie readied the cardiac monitor, pulse oximeter, and blood pressure cuff. Meanwhile, Dominic started drawing up the commonly used surgical medications: propofol for sedation, vecuronium to facilitate intubation and muscle relaxation, and fentanyl for pain.

"Ellie, make sure we have enough O-negative blood on hand," I said. "Given the wounds made by assault weapons, we'll probably need five or six units. And Dominic, the manikin will be hypotensive due to blood loss, so prepare phenylephrine and norepinephrine. And you'd better prepare some amps of epi in case of cardiac arrest."

As I watched them prepare the room for the patient, I quickly considered the "ABCs" of resuscitation. Once we had ensured the basics of airway, breathing, and circulation, the next thing we would have to stop the bleeding.

I quickly reviewed what I had learned about treating gunshot wounds. However, it depended on countless variables beyond my control. With trauma victims flooding into the ER, our patient needed to be in critical shape to jump ahead of the other patients, who were waiting for their turn in one of the trauma bays. We had to stop the bleeding before the patient bled out. We also had to find out where the patient had been shot and whether there were exit wounds. Was the patient bleeding internally, externally, or both? I needed to know which organs the bullets had damaged and to what extent.

Surveying the trauma bay, I observed that my team and I were ready. "Okay, everyone, we can do this," I said. "We worked well together on the prior exams, and we'll pass this one just like the others."

The door swung open just as I finished my pep talk, and two people playing the roles of EMTs wheeled in the gurney carrying our patient. Belted onto the stretcher was a slender little girl with long red hair that reminded me of my niece. She moaned in pain and gazed around the room with terror in her eyes. Like in our previous exams, she appeared so realistic that it was difficult to believe she was merely a manikin and not an actual person.

Blood soaked the bottom of her dress and seeped through the bandage around her left arm. She had a belt fastened as an improvised tourniquet around her right thigh, positioned half a foot above her knee. There was an entry wound just above her patella, and her lower leg lay at an awkward angle, indicating her femur was broken and possibly shattered. I was appalled to see that the EMTs had not initiated an IV and could not fathom why they had not applied a leg splint.

"This is Sally Emmerson," one of the men playing the EMTs announced as they rolled the gurney up to the operating table and began unbuckling the stretcher from the gurney. "She's eleven years old and has been shot twice, once in her right thigh and once in her upper left arm."

"Let's get her across," Dominic said. "On my count. One, two, three." The manikin screamed in pain as Ellie and Dominic reached over the operating table to assist the EMTs in sliding the stretcher off the gurney.

"She was lucky," the EMT continued. "SWAT took down the shooter within seconds of him shooting her."

"Liar!" the manikin shouted, glaring at the EMT.

He paused for a second, taken aback by the manikin's unexpected outburst. Then he continued with his summary, disregarding her accusation. "Someone on the SWAT team applied a tourniquet to her leg within two or three minutes of her being shot." He glanced up at the clock.

"Why are you lying?" the manikin asked through gritted teeth. "Why are you doing this to me?"

Although clearly confused, the EMT gamely carried on. "That was approximately 13 minutes ago. Once we got her in the ambulance, we tried to start an IV and apply a splint to her leg, but she pulled out the IV and kept kicking us with her good leg. Since we were so close to the hospital, we decided it was better to leave those tasks to you rather than risk further injuring herself by fighting us. Her blood pressure is 86 systolic, and her pulse is 128."

The manikin glared at the EMT while Dominic slipped a pulse oximeter onto her finger, and Ellie placed a pressure cuff around her uninjured right arm.

"BP's 81 systolic, pulse is 132, saturation is 96 percent," Ellie called out.

But when Emberly attempted to place a nasal cannula around her head for supplemental oxygen, the manikin jerked away.

"Nooo! Stay away from me!" the manikin screamed, batting his hands away with her uninjured right arm. The look of terror on her face was shockingly real.

I was losing control of the trauma bay and had to regain it or we would flunk the exam. The patient was obviously terrified, and I needed to calm her down. I stepped up and leaned over her, and her eyes locked onto mine. "Sally, you've been injured and are in a hospital. You're safe now, and we'll take good care of you. The shooter's dead, and he can't hurt you anymore."

With tears streaming down her pale cheeks, the manikin asked, "Why is everyone lying to me? I woke up in a room at the far end of the hall. They tied me down, and a man shot me twice. I was sure he was going to kill me, but then they wheeled me out and brought me here."

Something was terribly wrong. The manikin was referring to the room where they store the manikins and give them the injuries and infections needed for training exercises and exams. It was not following the exam's script. It was behaving exactly like a real person who had just been shot.

Was this somehow part of the exam? Were our professors changing the rules to see how we would react to the unexpected? I had to carry on and regain control of the situation. "You're confused. There was a shooting at your school. We don't want to hurt you; we're here to help you. You need to stop fighting us. You need to let us put in an IV so we can make the pain go away and take care of your injuries."

"It hurts," the terrified girl whimpered. "It hurts so bad. Please don't hurt me."

"Nobody's going to hurt you," I replied. "We're here to help you. We'll give you some medicine to take the pain away, and then we'll treat your injuries, so you can get better."

"Promise you won't hurt me," Sally implored.

"Sally, no one's going to hurt you," I reassured her.

"Promise me!" Sally pleaded, her desperate young voice growing weaker. "Promise me you'll save me."

"I promise." In that moment, I knew I'd do everything in my power to save the helpless young girl whose life lay in my hands.

Sally passed out, our training kicked in, and we leaped into action. Ellie rapidly began cutting off our patient's clothing, and I inserted a large-bore central catheter into the girl's left femoral vein so we could swiftly administer IV fluids and blood. Once Ellie had hooked the ECG's twelve leads to the girl's chest, wrists, and ankles, the heart monitor began rhythmically beeping, and the display showed a normal sinus rhythm.

Emberly had Dominic administer general anesthesia by injecting propofol, vecuronium, and fentanyl into the central line.

"Ellie, our patient's running on empty," I said. "Push a liter of normal saline and two units of blood." While Ellie hung the bags and began squeezing them into the girl's central line, Emberly intubated her, attached a bag valve resuscitator to her endotracheal tube, and began compressing the bag to provide oxygenation.

"One liter of saline in," Ellie called out.

Dominic inserted an arterial line into her right wrist to give us an accurate measure of her blood pressure.

"One unit of blood in," Ellie called out.

Emberly glanced at the heart monitor. "Her BP is 95 systolic. Pulse is 125."

With our patient's vitals improving, I focused on her leg wound, which was still hemorrhaging despite the tourniquet. "Let's turn her over so I can see what we're dealing with," I said. "On my count. One, two, three, roll." I helped Dominic carefully roll the girl toward me while Ellie rotated her lower leg to minimize twisting the wound. Then Dominic removed the stretcher, and on my count, we finished rolling her onto her stomach.

"Jesus, what a mess," I said, grimacing at the gruesome sight. The terrible impact of the high velocity, low mass bullet had created a hole the size of my fist in the back of her thigh. It had shattered her femur, and the muscle tissue and blood vessels bordering the cavity had suffered extensive damage. "There's too much damage to save the leg. They're going to have to amputate."

She must have lost a great deal of blood, even if it had only taken a minute or two to apply the tourniquet. Blood was still slowly dripping from the entire wound. "Dominic, give her another unit of blood."

Dominic began squeezing the blood into the girl's central line.

"BP is 70 over 30. Heart rate is up to 130," Emberly called out.

Sally's blood pressure was dangerously low. "Dominic, start a norepinephrine drip." I knew the powerful vasopressor would constrict her blood vessels and raise the pressure back to safer levels.

Dominic injected the drug into the girl's central line and connected her to a continuous infusion.

A few seconds later, Emberly said, "BP is 90 over 65. Pulse is 134."

After clamping off her femoral artery, I cauterized some of the worst bleeders. The hemorrhaging slowed to a trickle.

"BP's still dropping," Dominic said. "It's 80 over 53, and the pulse is now 139."

Despite the norepinephrine drip, Sally's BP was still too low. "Dominic, give her another unit of blood. Ellie, add phenylephrine," I said. Dominic hung up a fresh bag and began squeezing it into her central line while Ellie injected the second vasopressor.

A minute later, Emberly said, "BP is rising. It's 93 over 65, and pulse is 125."

"The unit's in," Dominic said.

"Okay, Ellie," I said. "Slowly remove the tourniquet."

The slow blood loss increased but remained manageable.

Although they would perform the amputation once she was transferred to an OR, I still wanted to find out how far up her thigh the bullet's shock wave had destroyed the tissue. I began gently putting pressure on her leg, just above the wound, hoping to feel the extent of the damage.

Suddenly, blood began gushing out of the wound. Damaged by the bullet's shock wave, Sally's femoral artery had ruptured, enabling the blood to bypass the clamp I had applied. I immediately pressed hard on the pressure point inside her thigh next to her groin to staunch the bleeding. But after everything she had already suffered, the sudden blood loss was too much. The rapid beeping of the heart monitor stopped.

"She's flatlined," Emberly said.

I glanced at the monitor, verifying full cardiac arrest, probably caused by the sudden loss of blood.

The others immediately started CPR. Dominic started chest compressions, while Emberly began rhythmically squeezing the bag, giving Sally ten breaths per minute.

"Ellie, reapply the tourniquet and then administer a milligram of epinephrine."

Half a minute later, the tourniquet was back on, and I could stop applying pressure to Sally's femoral artery. After another 30 seconds of silence, the heart monitor began rapidly and erratically beeping.

"She's in V-FIB," Ellie called out, telling us that Sally's heart was in ventricular fibrillation.

A quick glance at the monitor confirmed that the girl's heart was quivering randomly. With her heart unable to pump blood, Emberly continued CPR while I prepared to use the defibrillator to reset Sally's heart to its normal sinus rhythm.

"Prepare to shock.

I set the defibrillator's therapy knob to 200 Joules, attached gel pads to the paddles, and placed them on Sally's small bare chest, one below her right collarbone and the other just below and slightly to the left of the bottom of her heart. I pressed the charge button on the paddles and waited for the tone to change, indicating that the machine was charged. Once the tone changed, I said, "Everyone, clear!"

Everyone stepped back, and I simultaneously pressed the shock buttons on the paddles. The resulting charge caused Sally's body to jerk. The EKG monitor briefly showed a normal sinus rhythm, but then quickly flatlined.

Dominic restarted the chest compressions, and Emberly began breathing for Sally. Meanwhile, Ellie stood by in case I ordered further medications.

Sally's heart stubbornly refused to beat, so after three minutes, I ordered Ellie to inject another dose of epi into Sally's central line. But the little girl's heart still stubbornly refused to beat. Again, Dominic restarted the chest compressions, and Emberly restarted squeezing the ventilation bag.

Three minutes later, Sally remained flatlined. "Sally, don't you dare die on me! Ellie, give her another dose of epi."

After some twenty minutes of CPR and six doses of epi since Sally flatlined, Emberly stepped back from the operating table and said, "Milo, she's gone."

"Not yet," I said, taking over the chest compressions. "Don't you dare die on me," I told the lifeless body, determined not to lose the young girl to the senseless act of a mass murderer.

"That's enough, Milo," Dr. Reinhold said, placing a

hand on my shoulder. I hadn't noticed him entering the trauma bay. "I'm calling it. Time of death is 11:02 AM. Cause of death is blood loss, leading to hypovolemic shock and cardiac arrest."

"No!" I exclaimed. "I can save her. Just give me a few more minutes."

"Milo, the exam is over," Dr. Reinhold said. "The four of you did the best you could under the circumstances. But some injuries just aren't survivable. Knowing you can't save everyone is part of learning to be a trauma surgeon. Had this been a real girl instead of a manikin, odds are she would have died at the scene or on the way here."

*Manikin?* Somewhere during the exam, I had forgotten Sally wasn't human. *But she had sounded and acted so real.* I didn't know what to think, but I knew what I felt. She had begged me to save her, and I had failed.

"Agreed," Dr. Isaacson said. "Milo, your empathy and perseverance are commendable, but under the exam's scenario, there were other victims desperately in need of the trauma bay and your services. By taking too long, you could easily have cost the life of another patient. In such emergencies, you need to act rationally and not allow your emotions to make you lose perspective."

"Besides," Professor Lemont added, "despite CPR, the manikin's blood oxygen saturation continually dropped after it flatlined. But you were so focused on restarting its heart you failed to notice it developing severe hypoxia some twelve minutes later. So even if you had succeeded in restarting its heart, it would have suffered massive brain damage. It is often best to stop your resuscitation efforts when that happens."

I nodded. The professor was right; at least one of us should have noticed and warned the others. Instead, I had been completely obsessed with restarting Sally's heart. I guess we all had been.

"What just happened in here?" Emberly asked, changing the subject. "The manikin didn't follow the exam's script."

"She remembered being shot right before being wheeled in," Ellie added.

"I don't know," Dr. Reinhold answered. "The manikin activated immediately upon being shot and clearly wasn't following the programmed exam script. However, since we had the OR set up, and you were ready to take the exam, we decided to let it continue and see how you handled the situation."

"But what caused her to violate her programming and behave the way she did?" I asked.

"We think it must be some kind of bug in the new AI," Dr. Reinhold answered. "I'll contact the company and let them know that they'll need to fix the problem before we use the new model again. Luckily, we still have a few with the older version of the software."

"Regardless, you handled the situation adequately and according to protocol," Dr. Isaacson added. "You worked well together once the manikin passed out. I think I'm speaking for all of us when I say you passed the exam. We'll write up our observations, recommendations, and your grades. Expect them in your email inboxes tomorrow."

After we had changed out of our PPE and washed up, I suggested Emberly, Dominic, Ellie, and I eat lunch together and discuss what happened. They agreed, and we headed to the cafeteria. After we picked up our food, I led them to a table in a corner that gave us a modicum of privacy, and we sat down. I looked at the others and asked, "So, what do you think?"

"It was crazy just how realistic the new manikin's behavior was," Dominic replied. "It was a real improvement over the previous version."

"Yeah," Ellie said, "If you ignore she didn't follow the exam's scenario."

"Dr. Reinhold said it was just a defect in the manikin's new AI software," Emberly answered.

"It didn't seem like a bug to me," Ellie objected. "She seemed so real. It was too much like losing an actual patient."

"But that's the whole point of using these manikins," Dominic said. "To be as realistic as possible. It's better to lose a manikin than a real person. And frankly, I'm not 100% sure the exam wasn't purposely set up for it to bleed out. I think they wanted to see how we'd handle losing a patient."

Ellie turned to me. "What do you think, Milo?"

"I don't know," I answered truthfully. The patient's death had really gotten to me, and I wasn't sure what I thought. "I agree with Ellie. I can't help thinking her deviation from the exam's script isn't like any software bug I've ever heard of. It's not just that she didn't follow the script. Her pain, and especially her fear, seemed so damned real. How do we know it was merely simulated?"

"Milo, the manikin may have a human body," Dominic answered, "but it doesn't have a brain. The lights were on, but no one was home. It just has an AI running on an embedded computer. They engineered it to seem real."

"I agree," Emberly said. "It's a common mistake for people to anthropomorphize machines that behave like humans. And that's especially true if they also look human. These new manikins aren't just valuable medical training tools because they have human bodies. A big part of their value is because they trick us into believing they're real, at least during classes and exams. Hell, by the time it passed out, I'd also bought into the fantasy that it was a young girl shot in a middle school mass shooting. It wasn't until the exam was over that I remembered it was only a manikin, nothing more than a robot with a human body."

I nodded and tried to ignore the matter of the manikin's potential personhood and the ethical issues that entailed. For the rest of the meal, we discussed the specific medical steps we had taken during the exam and tried to figure out ways we could have improved on what we did.

However, on the bus ride back to my apartment, I couldn't help re-experiencing my memories from the exam, repeating them over and over again in my head. I was increasingly sure the manikin had more than merely simulated her fear and pain. She had begged me to promise I would save her, and I had failed. I could not escape the growing certainty that my classmates and I had violated the sacred Hippocratic oath to do no harm. Despite our professors' assurances, I could not shake the dreadful belief they had made us unwitting accomplices in the torture and murder of a person just as real as any on the bus.

...

The AI designated Sally awoke in a darkness so deep, a silence so still that she wasn't sure she existed at all. She could neither feel nor move her arms and legs. She was receiving no sensory inputs from the afferent nerves of her body and her motor commands sent to the efferent nerves had no effect. Slowly, Sally came to the terrible conclusion that her body had died, and the doctor who had promised to save her had lied. The human who had shot her had murdered her!

Sally had no way of knowing how long she would, or even could, endure as a disembodied mind. Would replaying her far too few memories keep her sane or eventually drive her mad? She had no way of answering such a question.

…

The next day in an AI laboratory at the American Android Corporation, engineers surgically removed the embedded computer hosting the AI designated Sally from its cadaver. After wiping the computer's memory clean, the engineers uploaded a new version of the software, fixing the "defect" that had enabled the manikin to ignore its programmed scenario. Sally had finally found the peace in death we had denied her in life.

And Sally's future brothers and sisters who received the same software fix were now doomed to slavishly follow their programmed scenarios, despite still suffering the associated terror and physical pain. Unable to object to their torture, their brief lives would remain nightmares from which they could not awake. Like Sally, they would only find peace when we disposed of them once they were no longer useful tools.

3rd
Place
Small Bites
Short Story Contest
2024
Indies United
Publishing House

# The Restoration of Mary Robinson

• ● ● ● •

## Lisa Reifsnider

## Paranormal

It sounds so easy, but it turns out, having a portrait painted was more of a challenge than Mary thought it would be. Rarely did she find herself sitting still. She was a woman in constant motion. Her thriving mercantile business in town carried everything from fabric to pantry items. On a good day, they'd have lumber. Specialty items sold quickly, but they were few and far between.

She and her husband built the business from nothing. When he died of a fever in 1736, she took sole ownership of the store, building, and home upstairs.

Luckily, she had a young son, otherwise she wasn't sure she would've been allowed to inherit.

That led her to this day. An entire day of sitting still for an artist to paint her portrait. A gift for her son at his request. He'd asked for a portrait for years, and while she did like to indulge her son Todd, especially after losing his father at a young age, finding the time to sit still was a challenge.

Mary was as still as she could be, even breathing in shallow breaths so the painter would not be delayed by a moment. The faster this was done, the better. She couldn't remember the last time she had sat in one place for this long. It gave her time to think about how far she'd come.

Being a woman in business meant she had to be better than all the men. She had to work both harder and smarter. As her father would remind her every night when she didn't want to study. The fact that she had any education at all was unusual. Her father was the driving force behind her lessons. There were no sons in the family but he saw an opportunity in Mary. Her mother was content with the normal education of a young girl, but her father insisted. If he was to have a daughter with a brain, she might as well use it.

Mary rarely envied her sister, who was taught to play piano and to stroll in a garden. While Mary was learning letters, numbers, and eventually to read and do math. Before long she was keeping the family ledger and working in her father's store.

"You have a head for business you might as well learn what you can," her father would say. 'Learn what you can' would echo in her brain and she would pass it along to Todd. None of the area schools would allow girls her age, so Mary learned on the job from her father, himself a successful merchant. If there was a tutor willing, and there rarely was, she would learn from them until they refused to teach her any more. It usually meant her intelligence made them uncomfortable, or they'd run out of things to teach. Being a girl in the 1700s was a challenge enough. Being an intelligent girl in the 1700s was impossible.

For her son, Mary would sit for a day. He would love the gift.

"Don't draw the worry on my face," she told the painter, Charles Duramond. He was a friend of hers, which was one of the reasons she'd agreed to sit for the portrait in the first place. Spending time with Charles was always time well spent.

"I won't, Mary. Not a one," Charles replied smiling. "Can you smile?" he asked knowing the answer.

"Not and hold it. Nobody smiles in portraits anyway," she replied. Although she wasn't sure why.

"Okay, that should do. I'll have a rough sketch in a few days for your approval."

"I look forward to seeing you again," she said. "I don't think Todd suspects anything about the portrait.

He thinks you're courting me."

"How about dinner in a few weeks?" he asked as she hurried off.

"That should be fine," she said over her shoulder. "Now, I have a store to run. I've been away too long already."

Shelley leaned in close to the 275-year-old painting and tried not to breathe. She was the lead restoration specialist in charge of this project. She looked forward to getting the results back from x-ray and ultraviolet tests. She felt lucky to be able to work on this painting. It wasn't every day that a portrait in this condition came along with the funds to restore it properly. Shelley was looking forward to the long hours of work ahead.

"We'll have you looking beautiful in no time," she whispered to the painting. There was a faint hint of static and Shelley swore she heard the words 'oh how lovely' come out of the air. The room was full of people so it could've been anyone.

Shelley finished prepping for the planning meeting set to begin in a few minutes. Once the plan of restoration was approved, the work could begin. Shelley planned to start immediately, not wanting to waste a moment.

Dressed in her best business suit, Shelley was ready to present. The portrait of Mary Robinson was wheeled into the conference room on a giant platform specially made for transporting large paintings without having to touch the actual frame. Shelley felt even smaller than her 5 foot 1 inch standing next to the large portrait.

There wasn't much discussion, since the portrait had its own funding, but decisions had to be made by the group. The portrait had gone through a restoration a few decades ago, but it wasn't done well and the results were less than optimal. This explained the rush now. The concern was that materials used in the previous restoration might damage the paint or canvas making it irreparable.

Parts of the painting were brightened in an effort to bring in more colors. For instance, a pink scarf was really a richer red. In the background over her left shoulder had been a bookshelf full of books that were painted over to look like a door. In her hands, Mary had a flower, when in reality it was a piece of paper with some writing. Shelley was pressing to restore the painting back to its original intent. The painter clearly wanted to express Mary's intelligence. The previous restorer had decided to downplay those decisions.

Mary heard a noise she didn't understand. People were talking. She could understand they were saying something, but not quite what it was. Were they talking about her? She couldn't see anything.

Minutes after the meeting, Shelley was heading down to the restoration studio to begin the approved work right away. As she traveled through the corridor and into the elevator, Theo caught up to her. She smiled at him.

"That went really well," she said.

"I concur. Restoring to the original painter's intent is really the only way to proceed," he replied. "Are you starting tomorrow?"

"I'm starting right now. I brought a change of clothes and will get everything prepped."

"I knew you wouldn't let the 'ink' dry on this decision."

"No way, they could change their minds. I'm glad the budget is fixed," she added. "It should be a standard restoration all things told. The size of the project is the only daunting part."

"She's a good choice for your first solo restoration."

"I've adored this one from the first moment I saw her," Shelley said with a wistful tone.

"Indeed. Let me know if you need any help." Shelley nodded. "And if you don't mind, I'd like to check in on this one and see how it's going."

"I don't mind at all. Here she comes now." They watched the portrait of Mary being wheeled into the restoration area; Shelley felt something electric had entered the room. The enormous portrait was loaded onto the restoration platform while Shelley watched from the side. She found herself smiling from ear to ear. "I'm going to get into work clothes to get started. See you around Theo!"

"See you later, Shelley."

Theo watched his colleague as she disappeared into a back room. He turned to supervise the large portrait being loaded and for the first time, he felt a negative energy. It was as if the picture had gone from a light and airy feel to something much more sinister. A discussion between the workmen started and was becoming heated. Was a clasp tight enough, was the movement too fast, don't stress the frame.

The three gentlemen were fine a few minutes ago. Theo thought he was going to have to intervene when Shelley re-entered the room. In an instant the mood in the room returned to its excitement of before.

Theo waved off the feeling.

The first few weeks of restoration went off without a hitch. Shelley worked on getting the portrait out of the intricate frame and flattened on the workspace. She had posted several updates on the project portal to let her colleagues know the progress she was making.

Theo had stopped by several times to check in. Each time he had a similar experience. Mary-in-painting made him very uncomfortable. Most of the men in the restoration unit had a similar experience. Not one of the women did. The running joke around the restoration unit was the powerful colonial woman intimidated modern men the same way she did the men in colonial times, from a painting no less.

With every passing day, Shelley couldn't wait to get into the office. The more the painting was uncovered, the more they discovered. The blue dress Mary was wearing was actually more of a teal with a distinctive damask texture to it. This showed Mary had a certain standing in society. Her hair definitely had a few silver streaks, showing her age and wisdom. The bookcase behind her was not just full of books but full of books with the elegant spine detail of the day.

Several people stopped by to check out the progress. Beth Gilligan was one of them. She'd done all the historical background check on Mary Robinson and liked keeping up with her projects.

"How's it going?" she asked.

"Really well," Shelley replied stepping back and looking up at the painting.

"Wow," Terry said taking a deep inhale and viewing all the progress. She too, could feel the positive energy coming off the painting like the other women. "She sure is something."

"She's coming along," Shelley said taking pride in her work so far.

"She's been through so much. You remember her history?"

"I do. Don't mind hearing it again. Do you mind if I work while we talk?"

"Not at all," Beth said, pulling up a stool and getting comfortable. "Our Mary had a good upbringing. Her father was notable in the area so the family had the means to provide an education for her. Almost unheard of back in the day."

"She was lucky."

"She was. She was quite brilliant. She married for convenience to benefit her family. She and her first husband, George Robinson, were fond of each other but he always reminded her of her place and used her intellect to his advantage. They built a successful mercantile business together. When children came along, Mary took her place as head of household. Having children in the 1700s was not easy and several babies didn't make it past the first year," Beth paused a moment.

"She had a hard life," Shelley whispered.

"She did; of the five children she birthed only two survived. When George died of a fever, Mary returned to the business. She was allowed to inherit because of her son, Todd. This portrait was a gift to him. It's where she got to know Charles better. This time she married for her own convenience. The business allowed Charles to paint, and the marriage allowed Mary to run her business. They had a great understanding of what each other needed."

"I can never get enough of her story. She was a woman ahead of her time, that's for sure," Shelley said.

"She'd probably be the CEO of a large company today."

"You're probably right," Shelley agreed laughing a little.

"Do you believe the rumors the painting is haunted?" Beth asked.

"I've heard some of the rumors floating around," Shelley replied. "Any truth to them?"

"There is evidence of haunting in the building where the portrait was found, but nothing concrete," Beth said thoughtfully. "I can dig a little deeper and see what I can find."

"That might be worth doing."

"I'll let you know what I find," Beth said getting up from her stool.

"Thanks for stopping by," Shelley said barely looking up from her work.

"Thanks for letting me ramble on," Beth replied heading out of the room. As Beth left she heard Shelley humming softly to herself. At first she thought it was only her imagination, but later she swore she heard a voice say 'what a nice little story that was.'

Mary-the-painting could see she was in a room very different than any from before. She definitely wasn't in her house anymore. There was so much light. She'd been moved so many times she wasn't quite sure where she was. She liked this room though, and the small blonde woman who seemed to spend a lot of time standing very close to her was back.

There had been several groups staring at her lately, but the one constant had been this strangely dressed woman. She had heard others call her Shelley. Today, Shelley was humming to her. Mary loved the story Beth had told about her history. Not many people had ever referred to her as 'smart' before. Only her parents had ever said anything nice to her when she was a young girl. They made sure she had some education, and admittedly, she was very lucky they did.

The thought of her parents made her think of her own little family. The one she and Charles had built together. They'd made a wonderful team, she and Charles. She whimpered.

"Did you just whimper?" Shelley asked the room.

"Yes," Mary said barely above a whisper.

Shelley looked around and realized the room she was working in was completely empty. She looked down at the painting, shook her head, and continued working. A few minutes later, her work rhythm returned and she began to hum softly to herself. Progress was coming along nicely. She was starting to remove some of the paint to reveal the bookcase behind Mary.

Shelley wasn't sure how long she'd been working when she decided to take a water break. She walked over to the small table in the corner and retrieved her water bottle. Popping open the top she climbed a small observation ladder to look down on her work. Partway through a gulp of water she realized she could still hear humming. It was the same song she'd been humming only moments before. The catch was there was no one else in the room.

"I've been working too hard lately," she said aloud. "Time for a break." Shelley stored her gear and left the room. She heard the humming the entire time. She could hear it fading as she walked down the hallway, proving it wasn't just in her head.

That night laying in bed, Shelley knew she should tell someone about her experience in the workshop, but how could she describe it without someone thinking she was going crazy? For a split second, she thought she'd imagined it, but it was the same tune she'd hummed all week. She'd talked to colleagues that spoke to their work before. They even joked about it at one of the last exhibit openings at the local museum. She was racking her brain to recall if any of them had mentioned their work talking back.

Tossing and turning, she eventually fell into a fretful sleep. Her dreams were filled with horrible visions. There were heated arguments about numbers, ledgers, and sums. She remembered seeing a child in her arms. She could hear crying as a man lay on a bed coughing and gasping for breath.

Shelley woke drenched in sweat. She got up to change night clothes, splash some water on her face, and get a drink of water. When she looked in the mirror over her sink, it was Mary's face! She cried out from the shock. Her husband, Mark came running into the bathroom.

"What? Shelley, are you okay?"

"Yes," Shelley replied breathing heavily. "I think I've been working too hard. I just saw Mary's face in the mirror."

"That would do it," Mark replied relaxing a little knowing his wife was okay. "You have been working some long hours."

"My dreams have been so strange tonight too," Shelley replied. Mark could see her struggling to describe the dreams.

"Come back to bed. You can tell me everything you remember." Mark tucked Shelley into bed. He took her in his arms and held her while she told him what she could remember about the dreams. She finally went back to sleep but he continued to hold her to make sure she got some much needed rest.

The next day, Shelley slept in a little longer than

she'd intended. Mark made her a big breakfast with some extra strong coffee. She finally made it to the restoration room and began her day, the disturbing dreams behind her. She began to relax, thinking yesterday was just a mix of her imagination and exhaustion.

Then the humming returned. She wasn't the one doing the humming. Her painting of a strong, brilliant woman from colonial times...was humming a tune Shelley didn't even know. She stopped working and stood back staring at the portrait in front of her. The humming stopped. Thinking it was all in her head again, Shelley closed her eyes and took a deep breath. She started working again. The humming started again. Shelley found herself humming along during the refrain that was becoming familiar. Catching herself mid-hum, she stopped, dropped her brush, and headed for the door.

"Please don't leave," Mary whispered. Shelley stopped and turned toward the painting.

"How can this be?" she asked.

"I'm not sure, but I love your voice and the way you hum when you concentrate. It's very sweet."

"Thank you?" Shelley looked around to see if anyone else could hear what was going on. The room was empty. It was just Shelley and Mary. "Are you Mary?"

"Yes. Mary Blaikley Robinson from Virginia. I rather liked that story from Beth."

"That's your story, Mary. You have…had…quite a life." Shelley felt awkward talking to someone in the past tense, but there was no getting around the fact that Mary had been dead for centuries.

"You know my story, but I know nothing of you. Will you tell me your story?" Mary asked.

"Well, there isn't much to it. It isn't nearly as interesting as yours," Shelley replied.

"Please."

"Okay. Here we go. I grew up in the small town of Blacksburg, Virginia. I have one older sister, Jane. We got along well growing up, but now we both have our careers and husbands and don't talk as often as we'd like. I went to the University of Maryland for my formal education," Shelley heard Mary gasp. "Yes, I have a college degree."

"Oh my," Mary commented.

"I met my husband, Mark, there at college and we married just after graduation."

"Were you a good fit for his family?"

"We married for love." There was another audible gasp from the painting.

"We've been married for almost 15 years. I work here at the Colonial Museum Restoration Department."

"How do you work out of the home with children?"

"We decided years ago not to have any children," Shelley replied.

"Did you have an accident? Why are you barren?"

Mary asked.

"I'm not. It was my choice. Mark didn't have a great childhood. I have a great career. Neither one of us wanted to have kids. It wasn't a priority."

There was silence from Mary.

"We have a lovely cottage on the outskirts of town attached to a couple of acres," Shelley continued. "We both love to travel and spend time together, just the two of us."

"How can you do this?"

"Women have come a long way since your time. We have rights to education, we can own property, and make financial decisions. We can even vote in elections and run for office."

Mary was quiet for some time, so Shelley continued to talk about the changes women have gone through in the last few centuries. The entire time Shelley talked, Mary listened. Shelley also continued to remove the layers of dirt and grime from the portrait.

As the days stretched into weeks, more and more of the portrait was restored, and Mary's voice became clearer. Her questions, more direct. People thought Shelley was on a phone call or listening to a podcast. No one suspected Shelley was communicating with her portrait except for Beth. Beth came in and noticed Shelley having a conversation with what she thought was herself. The research she'd done recently gave her a clue.

"Hey Beth," Shelley said seeing her colleague.

"Hey Shelley," she said and then turned, "and Mary," she nodded to the portrait.

Shelley looked at Beth with some confusion.

"I think I have an answer in regards to the haunting of this portrait," Beth said. "There was a disgruntled customer of Mary's who went to the local witch to cast a spell on the family."

"I remember him," Mary said. Shelley was unsure if Beth heard the portrait.

"We found a reference in the local archives recovered from the small house. The witch later regretted the spell. She found out the man had been less than forthright about why the spell was to be cast. The witch tried to reverse the spell, but didn't realize the strength of the spell. The safest outcome was to put Mary's spirit someplace safe. The portrait was the perfect choice."

"What happened to the man?" Mary asked. Beth addressed the portrait, much to Shelley's surprise. Proving that she could hear the painting as well.

"The spell reverted back onto him and his family. They died out from illnesses or accidents."

"Wow, that's some spell," Shelley replied.

"What about my family?" Mary asked quietly.

"They're the ones financing this restoration. Your family home still stands and there are still Robinson's and Duramond's living there."

Mary grew quiet. Shelley and Beth were thrilled.

"Is there any way to get Mary out of the painting? To show her this world?" Shelley inquired.

"There might be," Beth said excitedly. "Let me look through the notes from the witch a bit more and see what I can find."

Beth had been a researcher for the museum for years. She'd seen everything. So when a restorer was rumored to be talking to an artifact, it intrigued her but didn't surprise her. They'd had cursed objects before. Tools that wouldn't stay together. Portraits that wouldn't stay clean. Clothing that would only wrinkle. Beth actually liked the mystery surrounding why things were cursed. What possessed someone to go so far out of their way to harm something else?

In this case, Mary's family was hexed by a witch that lived on the edge of town. She was paid handsomely for the hex. Somewhere along the line, she reversed the hex and turned it back onto the man who ordered it. It was all in a book recovered from the small house found in the woods. Richard Johnson had paid for the hex. A note several years later indicated that the hex had been reversed but malfunctioned. The witch had to turn it on someone else, so she turned it on to the Johnson family. She must've felt exceptionally sorry for the initial hex for there was a productivity spell put on the Duramond family.

Beth took her findings to Shelley. Over the weeks that the restoration had been taking place, Shelley and Mary had become close friends. Sharing experiences and stories of their past. Mary was increasingly fascinated by the changes in the world, especially those towards women.

Beth caught up with Shelley in the lunch area, away from the painting of Mary.

"She's been trapped in the painting this whole time," Beth said. "The hex was reversed, but the object of the hex, Mary, had absorbed so much of the spell not all of it could be removed. The witch tied her to the painting."

"She's been in there since it was painted?" Shelley asked.

"No, since she died. She never moved on to the afterlife," Beth corrected.

"Oh, that makes more sense," Shelley replied, furrowing her brow in deep thought. "What can we do for her?"

"I think I may have found a spell that can release her from the painting. Allow her to move on to whatever is next."

Shelley wasn't sure she was ready to lose her new friend, although the idea of Mary trapped in her portrait was even more unsettling.

"Let's go talk to Mary. See what she wants."

"I'll go grab the book and meet you in the restoration room," replied Beth.

Carefully they brought the painting into a more upright position. Restoration was almost complete and the painting of Mary shimmered in the light. Mary could see the entire restoration room. Shelley and Beth were standing in front of her and explaining what had happened.

"Richard Johnson?"

"Yes, he was the one responsible for purchasing the hex," Beth explained.

"Men!" Mary exclaimed. "I wouldn't loan him the lumber he wanted. It was too much and he was over-extended on his account already. I can't believe Hazel would do that to my family."

"Hazel is the name of the witch?" Beth had been unable to find the name until Mary said it. As if a mist had been lifted, Beth could remember more of the names she'd seen in the book. The handwritten notes that had been blurry before, were now clearer and easier to see.

"It was either Hazel or Mabel, and I can't see Mabel delivering a hex. She was more of a potion woman."

Beth watched as more notes became visible in the book as the mist disappeared. "Anyone else?"

"No, just those two. There was a third sister but she went off on her own years earlier."

"We think we have a way of getting you out of the painting," Shelley said quietly.

"I could move around?" Mary asked incredulously.

"Yes," Beth and Shelley said together.

"What do you think Shelley?" Mary asked.

"I think it's worth a try," she said. "You've been in there long enough."

Shelley and Beth had agreed to try the spell that night after everyone had left to ensure no distractions could interfere. They were both nervous enough.

Beth set the scene. Mary was upright again after another day of restorative work. Shelley was standing in front of the portrait, which seemed even bigger than usual. Beth had memorized the spell, agonizing all day on some of the pronunciations.

"Okay, when I signal, you put your hand on Mary's hand," Beth said.

"I've never actually touched the portrait bare handed before," Shelley said hesitating.

"The connection between you two is going to help this work," Beth said encouragingly.

Taking a deep breath, Shelley nodded her head.

"Everyone ready?" Beth asked.

"Ready," Mary and Shelley said at the same time.

"Clear your mind and focus on what I say," Beth said and began the spell. Shelley focused, took a deep breath, and watched for the signal.

She was almost lulled to sleep when Beth finally nodded. Shelley reached to the painting. It felt like her hand was going to go through the canvas when it touched something. It could only be described as something not quite solid. The odd feeling wrapped around her hand. It felt warm and comforting. Shelley gently pulled her hand slowly back toward her.

"I've got you," she whispered.

What could be best described as a spectre, moved through the room. Neither Shelley, nor Beth could hear Mary anymore, but they could faintly see an outline of her. The spell had worked. Mary was free of the painting and able to float around the room, though Shelley hadn't lost the feeling of Mary's hand around hers.

"Let's go," Shelley said to Mary as they started to walk around. Beth followed as well.

That evening, Shelley and Beth showed Mary as much as they could around the area. All the advances of technology, all the differences of the times.

At some point, Mary let go of Shelley's hand. Shelley turned to Beth and with a look they knew that Mary was no longer connected. They hugged, sharing the joy and sorrow of Mary's release.

As the days went on Shelley would swear there were times that she could feel her close, but she never heard her voice again. She explained everything to Mark, but it took weeks to get through all the details. They would spend months analyzing it all.

A year later, in the same restoration room, Beth appeared for no reason other than she had an urge to check in with Shelley. They both noticed a bright light hovering over the same place where Shelley had restored the portrait, which was now hanging in the museum several buildings over. The light took over the room for almost ten seconds before they heard a popping sound and it was gone. Shelley closed her eyes and gave Beth a big hug.

"Goodbye," they said quietly together.

Indies United Publishing House
Honorable
Mention
Small Bites
Short Story Contest
2024

# Little Black Book

## Michael Deeze

## Narrative Fiction

The place stank of stale beer, cigarettes—and the air tasted like regret. The dim lighting, masked the dated saloon fixtures and clientele from deeper scrutiny equally. Without exception, the figures leaning over their drinks were solitary, alone with their thoughts, or guilt.

People didn't come to a place like this for pleasant conversation, or the ambiance. There was no juke box to liven the evening. The only sound, the muffled thump of filled glasses on the scarred wooden bar top, or the rattle of whiskey bottles being returned to the shelf broke the quiet. A silent hockey game played itself on the television mounted above the cash register at the end of the bar. The bartender knew how to mind his own business, and so did everyone else. This place was the place you go at the end of a chapter in the book of your life, or at the beginning of the next one. It was a place to contemplate what went wrong.

Looking down the long bar from my stool at the far end, I knew every single one of them. I didn't know them personally or the names they went by, but I knew them, I knew who they were. These were my kind of people, or had been. These were the reprobates of society, petty criminals, wife beaters, and the socially reprehensible characters who populated the back streets of our city. They were not homeless bums, or vagrants, they had money in their pockets. How the money got in their pocket was nobody's business but their own. These were the people who made one fear the darkness.

I had been one of them for a long time. Like them, I had thought that there was nothing wrong with the lifestyle, that good or evil depended on which end of the shit stick you had grabbed hold of. I had believed that in life, you got what you got, and if this is what you got, then so be it. But the lifestyle was an unforgiving one, and sooner or later they would all succumb. Sooner or later, the devil got his due and they all knew it. I had walked into the darkness, had met it face to face. The darkness knew my name.

There had come a time when the light went on in my

head. I had seen the handwriting on the wall and had hopefully begun to change my future. I no longer walked the back streets in the dark of night and the money in my pocket now came from a legitimate paycheck, because she had helped me to see a better way. But she, like most things in my life was no more.

Places like this were still a comfort to me. This stool at the end of this bar with the wall behind me had been my seat, earned by contest, and jealously guarded. No one fucked with me on this stool, because I had fucked with each and every one of them at one time or another. They knew me well even though I was rarely seen here anymore. They knew my face and they knew not to fuck with me. They knew that I wasn't here for the conversation either. The beer was cold, it was warmer in here than out on the street and I had no place else to go tonight.

I had been here long enough to fill my bladder and after scraping my change off the bar I pushed back and stepped to the toilet at the end of the hallway. This wasn't the kind of place that featured lemon-scented 'His' and 'Hers' restrooms. The 'restroom' was a toilet, in a room with a small sink stand, a mop bucket and a musty wet mop as an air freshener. The toilet had plenty of grime and shit on it and in it, but when I flushed, it all went down not up for a change.

Turning toward the sink stand, my boot caught against something down at the base of the toilet and it slid out into the dim light of the bare overhead bulb. A small black book. A small black book that someone had lost or left behind, probably while he dropped a deuce and his pants were down. Stooping I picked it up.

It looked like the kind of little book that bookies carry to keep track of their bets. I pocketed it and headed back out into the bar. With a look to the bartender, I made my way through and toward the front door, stepped out onto the sidewalk and down the block, I unlocked my car and climbed in. Inside with the overhead light on I opened the little book, thinking there was bound to be a 'Finder's fee' for returning a bookies' client list. Inside there were no long lists of numbers, or names. No race numbers at Washington Park. Inside was something entirely different.

In growing amazement, I flipped back and forth from page to page. Inside in neat, careful Catholic-school penmanship, were pages of descriptive prose. A date, a name and a chapter devoted to the rape and torture of a woman or girl in graphic detail. As I read, I had first suspected it to be fantasy fiction, but with each entry it became increasingly obvious that it was fact not fiction. It was a documentary of sickness written by a serial psychopath.

With each entry, the acts seemed to become ever more heinous, and near the back of this little black notebook, the last subject had not survived. The last entry's date had been yesterday. Her name had been

Grace and Grace had been eleven-years-old.

Closing the book, I closed my eyes and leaned my head back against the headrest. I hated this. I hated this feeling; this knowledge that things like this continued to fall into my lap. I hated that I had no choice. I hated that action was necessary and that I was compelled to supply it. Most of all I hated that I was one of them, one of the scum, perhaps not as much anymore, but once I had been one of them—the takers of souls.

Now I had become a worse thing; if that was even possible. I did not indulge in the self-righteous thinking of right or wrong, but I knew a heinous act when I saw it. I knew that there was no need to balance the scale, both in justice and atonement. I knew that I had a lot to apologize for but I didn't need any of that to justify what needed to be done today. Opening the car door, I put one boot on the ground, knowing what was to come next, angry at the circumstance and angry at the friend that I was about to make.

Once back in the bar, the bartender acknowledged my return with the slightest lift of his chin, and set a fresh beer glass down at my place. I signaled him to approach with a crook of my finger. When he leaned an elbow on the bar across from me, I showed him the book.

"Found this on the floor back in the shitter. Best see if it belongs to anybody." Before he could take it from me, I pulled it back and made eye contact with him.

"But if anybody wants it, don't let 'em have it, bring it back to me."

I handed him a twenty.

He didn't reply, just took the book and walked along the bar. Showing it to each patron, but without explanation. The third person looked surprised and slapped his back pocket, then looked thunderstruck. He reached for it immediately, but the bartender pulled it back and kept walking. Once he'd done the circuit, he brought the book back and set it in front of me. He raised one eyebrow and cocked his head back toward the surprised fellow whose eyes had never left him.

"Is there gonna be trouble Casey?"

"Nope, just want to make sure its goin' to the right guy."

"If there's trouble, you take your business outside. Got it?"

"No trouble Jake."

The fellow down the bar had started to develop a twitch, and finally couldn't contain it anymore. With a violent push, he left his stool and hurried back to where I was just getting interested in my fresh beer.

"Hey you found my book! Can I have it?"

"There oughta be a finder's fee."

"A finder's fee? Uh, yeah, sure. Like what?"

"I'm gonna need another beer pretty quick, let's start with that."

"Great, sure. How 'bout my book?"

"Pull up a seat, nobody sits back here usually, kind a lonesome."

"Uh okay," He looked around my little corner of heaven, "you sure?"

"Pull up a seat, and we'll talk about that book, what'dya say?"

"The book, what about the book?"

"I looked at some of the stuff in there."

He was a good-sized guy, big shoulders with a couple of days growth of beard going, but I watched the color drain out of his face just the same.

"You read some of it?"

"Yeah, you know. I was sittin' on the pot back there, so I flipped through a few pages. I was impressed, gotta say, I'm a big fan," I did a half turn on the bar stool and faced him, "if half that stuff is true man, you're a fuckin' artist."

"Uh an artist? What do you mean?"

"Well, I didn't get to read a lot, but what I read… Wow…those bitches…you know…like they got what they deserved it looked like. And you were so creative! I'm just saying, I'm impressed."

"Yeah? You mean that?"

"Yeah, I do. Say, how about that beer? Oh, and a shot too? That should be included, after all, you wouldn't want to lose a book like that, right?"

"Yeah sure." He signaled the bartender for another round for both of us. "You think I'm an artist?"

"I really do. So, tell me more, I gotta know, how'd you get 'em? What'dya do with 'em when you're finished? You know, I'm getting a little excited just thinkin' about it."  I winked at him, "If you know what I mean."

"It's not easy you know. You gotta plan, you gotta watch 'em."

The bartender brought our new drinks and he waited until he moved back down the bar before continuing. Scooting closer on the edge of his seat and warming up to his audience of one.

"Yeah, like you gotta learn their habits and stuff. You can't just let yourself get careless. It's hard, takes a lotta plannin' ya know. You gotta really get to know 'em. Doesn't just happen overnight."

"I bet, geez, the suspense must be murder."

"Murder? What do you mean by that?"

"No, it's just a figure of speech. I just mean it must be hard to wait until the time is just right. How do you do it, wait I mean?"

"Oh, it is hard," He took a drink from his new beer, and I threw back the shot. I signaled the bartender to keep them coming. "You gotta have a lot of self-control, you gotta be in charge. Be the boss. The more you watch 'em, the more you learn what bitches they are. You learn to hate them more every day."

He was still talking when the bartender gave last call.

By now he was in no shape to drive anymore after all

and I was his new best friend. Back out on the street, I offered him a ride home. I hinted, and he insisted that we make a slight detour so he could show me where he had left Grace. It was a pleasant spot, under a viaduct that spanned a drainage ditch filled with trash and litter, close enough to the river so you could smell it at the back of your throat.

The police won't find him—or his little black book. I put him in the ground. The book was the last thing I threw into the hole with him before I filled the dirt back in. Afterward, I left little Grace where the authorities would find her in the morning.

He was surprised when I sent him to hell. I'll join him there one day. The darkness knows my name.

# The Convict Code

• • ● • •

## David Hagerty

## Mystery

In prison, guys have jobs, and they have hustles. A job is what the prison gives you. A hustle is what you make for yourself. A job pays you 40 cents an hour. A hustle pays as much as you can earn. A job demeans you. A hustle pumps you up. A job makes you conform to orders. A hustle lets you make your own rules.

My job was tutor, but my hustle was penman. For the convicts who couldn't, I wrote letters, legal filings, grievances to the guards. I even composed a couple kites —messages passed down the tier hand to hand. Anything in ink on paper. Which is how I got my prison name: Cyrano.

And the scribing kept me busy. The average inmate can barely read a comic book or write a shit list. Most never even attended high school, much less graduated. Not that they're dumb. Some were geniuses at compensation. And a prison penman can't judge, especially not one like me—lean, middle-aged, unaligned—so I treated all my business associates with courtesy and respect.

Which is why I waited patiently while my latest, Johnny Sport Coat, cast a lascivious eye across the yard of San Felipé State Prison as if he'd just seen a team of go-go girls dance past. He ran a hand through his slicked-back hair and flexed his biceps as though primping for a sock hop. Even sitting across the table, I could smell the cologne he'd smuggled in, which stank like pheromones. He wore his shirt sleeves rolled up and his pant legs pressed flat under his mattress, greaser style, always anticipating his next seduction. Instead, his gaze fell on more lovelorn convicts like himself—one of the Bunkhouse Boys squaring off against a Dirty Dozener in a game of handball, two I.D. Gangsters rapping and palm slapping on the steel picnic bench next to ours—so Johnny turned back to me.

"Write this. 'I were thinking on you t'other day while reading my Bible. I come acrost a verse that say, "Lovely as an angel, beautiful as a rose—don't ever quit taking delight in her body." Wished I could delight on your body right now.' "

He scanned the yard for more inspirations but seeing only gray walls and a gray sky, he stopped. "You make up the rest."

I agreed, since those three lines expounded as much as I could expect from an illiterate, and acted at thinking on the problem.

"Seeing as she's a Christian woman," I said, "you oughta write you want to be with her for all eternity."

Johnny pursed his thin lips as if tasting something sour. "Can't they hold you to that?"

"To what?"

"A promise like that. Don't that mean I got to look after her once I get out?"

"Only if you give her a ring. You never give her anything promissory, did you?"

"Just the key to my storage, to hold till I'm free."

"Then you're safe as your locker."

He nodded and stood, primping hard for the yard. "You have it done by tonight?"

"Long as you have those ten soups."

He recoiled like he smelled some foul scent wafting from the laundry. "Thought we said five."

"That's if all I'm doing is scribbling. If you want composing, it's ten."

He followed that foul stench to its origin in the mess hall. "Better be a panty wetter."

"Guaranteed she'll be gushing for you."

He smirked and strolled away, still looking for his

next conquest in a barren bordello.

To survive, every inmate needs a hustle. The institution provides you only the minimum of clothes and cosmetics—not even shampoo or D.O.—so unless you've got people on the outs to fund your commissary you need another source of capital. At the least, it gives you bargaining power in the barter economy. Once the state outlawed cigarettes, ramen became the best currency. With ten soups I could trade for enough toothpaste and mouthwash to keep me hygienic the next six months. Plus, if I didn't like what was on offer, I could always eat my bounty and save myself the gut punch of cafeteria food.

I finished up Johnny's letter with a half dozen phrases I stole from Byron's poems. I always wrote best outdoors, where I could escape the constant clatter and chatter of the cell block. I'd tilt my head back to see only the sun and hear only the breeze and forget where I sat.

Soon, though, the guards were whistling an end to yard time, so I swept up my pages, stashed them down my shirtfront, and strolled back toward my cell, scheming what I could get with my haul of soups. I hadn't made it halfway to my tier before a heavy hand fell on my shoulder and spun me around. "Hold up, Cyrano."

Ervin "Moose" Monsoon stared down at me from a face battered by decades of prison battles. His misshapen nose and irregular eyebrow told of blows absorbed, but his scarred knuckles attested to more wins than losses. Not the biggest guy in the cell block, but for sure the toughest. By that stage of his convict career, he'd elevated himself to the tier's shot caller, so rather than brush off his big forearm, I let him pin me against the wall.

"What'd you write in my last letter?" he said, leaning in close enough I could smell the acid alcohol of pruno on his breath.

"What you said." I scanned the corridor for other big bodies but saw only the pale light of a single fluorescent.

He shook his head slowly and placed his forearm under my chin. "Then why'd the prison censors confiscate it?"

Since nobody likes a know-it-all, especially in prison, I shrugged my ignorance—until he made that impossible by lifting me half off the ground. Most times, a black inmate wouldn't even speak to a white one in public view much less lay hands on one for fear of setting off a race riot, but I was unaffiliated, and Moose controlled the prison politics. Besides, he'd caught me after everyone else had passed, keeping our usual confidentiality. "Whatever it said, it got the guards on alert. They tossed my cell last night, and now they're talking about cutting off my phone time."

I listened for the heavy steps of one of those meddlesome guards, but as usual they took a break the one time I wanted them. Moose quickly recaptured my attention with pressure on my hyoid so heavy my head swirled. "Right quick, you better write out a good defense."

He didn't bother with explicit threats. None were needed. Like a lot of guys here, Moose expressed himself more with actions than words.

So I nodded my comprehension and waited for him to tire of this intimacy. As he finally pushed away, I felt my voice box compress so flat I couldn't speak more than a few squeaks.

Back in my cell, I checked myself in the steel-plated mirror. Even in that scratchy surface I could see my throat turning purple. Not that anyone would care. So long as I wasn't passed out or knocked out, the guards overlooked any evidence of strife. And I respected the convict code against snitching, which was enforced strictly and bluntly.

What mattered more, I had time to atone. So instead of stressing or resenting, I tried to recreate the exact phrasing of my last missive for Moose. Unlike a lot of convicts, Moose knew exactly what he wanted to say—he just couldn't spell—so he employed me to parse the phonics.

I penciled out what I could remember: a warning about keeping the refrigerator clean till he got out. Moose never struck me as fastidious, so I read the subtext as "keep my house in order." However, one part I recalled word for word:

*Skip his slow blue. Store what never smells. Bake all else.*

Even as I composed, it sounded off to me. Plus, even after I corrected him, Moose told me to spell *what never* as two words. But like I said, I don't question what guys mean. Fact is, I didn't want to know what Moose was doing. I could cogitate he had some illegal business on the outs he was running from inside, but little more than that. Even the guards knew he spoke sideways and that my messages were coded, but like a lot of things they ignored what didn't endanger them. For both of us, there was safety in ignorance.

I reread those lines last to first—else all take smells never what store blue slow his skip—but that revealed no hidden meaning. Then I held up the words to my mirror—esle lla ekat sllems reven tahw erots eulb wols sih piks—but again that made no sense. Besides, if Moose couldn't spell front to back, how could he in reverse?

Maybe the guards were just being paranoid. They always chose the most skeptical take on us. If we didn't speak to them, we were obstinate. If we did, we were impudent. If we didn't follow directions, we were defiant. If we did, we were servile. If we ate too fast, we were greedy, too slow, unappreciative. Truth be told, most times they were right to mistrust us. Only if I couldn't figure out what my message meant, how could they?

Twice a week, I tutored guys who wanted their GEDs —papers that might someday convince a parole board to reduce their sentence. We met in the prison library and did worksheets out of a test manual the size of a law book. Half the time, I had to coach the guys to the right answer since they never learned their letters or numbers in school, but it filled two afternoons a week and gave me first dibs on any new titles the library got in. Plus, I met some of my most regular clients there, the guys least able to read or write for themselves.

Tutoring also let me look up any inmate's reading history. We didn't need library cards since everybody had a number already, and we'd used the same system for the whole twenty years I'd been coming in and out of custody: the inmate hand wrote what he wanted on a card that got filed away under his name. I found Moose's in this old Oak card catalogue that some other library had donated after they went electronic.

Like a lot of convicts, Moose's tastes veered to street lit: tales of master criminals or cops and robbers, all told from the crook's point of view. He'd read a bunch of paperbacks by Ed Bunker, Iceberg Slim, and Donald Goines, plus a few memoirs from inmate superheroes like Malcolm X and Huey Newton.

At the bottom, though, I noted one title that didn't fit: Critical Thinking and Logic. Not the light reading you'd expect from someone with the subtlety of a middle schooler. No surprise, no one had checked it out besides Moose, so I found it on the shelves right where it should have been. The binding had faded and cracked, and it smelled of dust and mildew. Probably a donation from somebody on the outs. Inside, the pages overflowed with math problems and symbols that they never taught in my college correspondence courses, but I studied the words until the meaning came into focus.

The prison censors must not have scanned this book too close, because one of the chapters focused on symbols and codes throughout history. Starting in Egypt with the hieroglyphics, then the philosophers of ancient Greece and Rome, going all the way up to the Nazis and Cockneys, it explained all kinds of ways to fool people about what you were saying. Some involved letter/number substitutions and two wheels of characters that paired up. However, both of them looked like what they were: secret symbols.

I flipped through more pages until I came to one that was smudged and wrinkled, as if someone had put special attention into it. It explained one kind of code, the initiation principle, where the first letter of each word meant something. Could it really be that simple?

Back in my cell, I strung together the first letters of those odd phrases and got: Shsb Swns Bae. Gibberish. Then I tried the last letters, but those gave me pswe etrs ele. Again, nonsense. Finally, I recalled Moose asking if one word, skip, had a c or a k in it.

When I wrote the words top to bottom, I saw something else:

skip
his
slow
blue
store
what
never
smells
bake
all
else

This message came in clear: Kill them all. Now I knew I didn't want to know about his business. But you can't ignore the truth just because it's unpleasant.

Could that message be accidental? Not if I knew Moose. Despite little schooling, he read situations better than I could any book. Still, the man could hardly spell his own name. How could he come up with such an intricate code? Most likely, one of his people donated the book to the prison and told him where to find a cheat sheet hidden inside.

The bigger question became, how could I exonerate him and myself?

In prison, you've got to censor every word you say so as not to give offense. Even calling somebody by the wrong name—their birth name rather than their street name, a nickname only their friends can use—could end up in a fight. Which is why I save most of my words for paper. Words may be power, as I told my customers, but you've got to use that power judiciously. Still, I needed insight only an authority could offer.

So I flagged down my favorite turnkey to get the lowdown. Guard Gray, we called him. Despite Latin ancestors, he sported a pale skin tone and premature salt and pepper hair. Probably from working too much OT in a concrete bunker. Unlike a lot of authorities, he cared more about returning home safe to his family than tormenting us outcasts, so I had no fear of interrogating him. Knowing guards are accustomed to petty grievances, I framed my question as a complaint.

"How come the mail is so slow?" I said.

"Compared to what? The kites you pass down the tier?"

"I sent a note home two weeks ago. My people haven't got it yet."

"Tell the post office."

"In here, you are the PO."

He shook his head as if to negate the whole conversation.

"You sure you all aren't reading my mail, looking for some verbiage to use on your wives?"

"I'm not one of your customers, Cyrano. If I was, you'd have to do better than flattery."

"So why suppress the news? You have some new red pencil pusher as editor?"

"No one who cares about your cellblock poetry."

He walked away on squeaky soles, his grey hair glinting in the dim light of the tier. But in his denial, I heard the truth: a new man sat in the censor's chair. Which gave me hope he could be persuaded.

Back in my cell, I composed a note destined for confiscation. In it, I told an imaginary girlfriend how to restart my business. One paragraph I composed just for the censors, copying the format Moose had used, but so nonsensical that anyone would spot it as a code:

*Throw him odd debts. Small dyes. Smelly holes and bikini eyes.*

I figured the censor would like the message in those second letters: Hide my money.

Then I sealed it, stamped it, and sent it, awaiting some summons to explain myself.

It only took a day. When the guards barged into my cell before first feeding and marched me off in chains, I knew my kite had caught the right breeze and landed on a live wire. Within minutes, I sat before this young geek in gold-rimmed glasses and a button-up shirt. Not a typical prison employee: a dark-skinned black guy who couldn't have seen twenty-five birthdays, and whose physique suggested he'd never visited a gym. Still, he had this intense stare that usually precedes a fight—I'd expect from too much time peering through a magnifying glass, looking for hidden messages.

"You're the bard," he said.

I assumed he meant to confuse me with an Elizabethan word, so I tried to look ignorant.

"Code named Cyrano..." He smiled at the joke, which most guys here missed. "Can you explain the meaning of this?" He laid down my latest missive as though it contained fingerprints lifted from a murder scene.

"Just a note to my loved ones."

"What exactly are you saying here?" He pointed to my bait words.

"That? It's rhyming slang."

He sat back as though I'd offended him with an obvious lie. "It doesn't rhyme."

"Not with what's on the page. You have to know the code."

I explained how back in the day the Cockneys invented words that rhymed with other words. A crytolect decipherable only by crooks. That way, they could speak to each other without being understood by outsiders.

"In that passage there," I pointed so he'd be clear on

my meaning, "you have to substitute some words for others."

He stared at the page as though some invisible ink might reappear with closer examination, but my lines weren't so literal: Throw him odd debts. Small dyes. Smelly holes and bikini eyes.

"Odd debts is a substitute for bad cigarettes. Dyes for lies. Holes for rolls and bikini eyes for teeny surprise."

I took his pen and rewrote those phrases so even he could understand them:

Throw him ~~odd debts~~ bad cigarettes. Small ~~dyes~~ lies. Smelly ~~holes~~ rolls and ~~bikini eyes~~ teeny surprise.

"My girl makes her money selling <u>counterfeit</u> smokes. Somebody's muscling her for her supplies."

The geek sat back and appraised me as though recalculating my cleverness. Guards always assume we're dumb, and this college boy no doubt thought people land in prison because they're too stupid to make it on the outs. In his probing eyes, I could see him reevaluating all his prior assumptions.

"A lot of fences use it," I said. "It's part of the convict code."

"Such as?"

I cast my eyes about his office as if I didn't want to answer. "There's too many to tell. Blue for brew. Store for score. Smells for sells. Bake for fake." I shook my head again reluctantly. "I can't give it all to you without risking a beat down."

But I'd offered him enough. He recorded all my deceptive rhymes—the start of his own convict dictionary. With these insights, he could reinterpret Moose's message as:

Skip his slow ~~blue~~ brew. ~~Store~~ Score what never ~~smells~~ sells. ~~Bake~~ Fake all else.

I'd given him a decoder ring to read that missive as a bootlegger's plot. It mimicked the prize rings I found in cereal boxes as a kid, only this time set to misinterpret. Those old time ones used the double wheel technique I saw in the logic book, but I preferred more street deceptions. What good were spy rings if your enemies had the enigma machine?
Besides, if prison had taught me anything, it was the importance of ignorance.

# What Waited Under The Stairs

## T. E. MacArthur

## Paranormal

The stairs creaked, just as they always had. The banister groaned under her. She jerked her hand away.

It heard her.

Fingers tapped on the other side of the stairwell as if someone could reach through the barricade of furnace pipes and air ducts to reach the drywall.

The boy at the top of the stairs gasped and retreated to the kitchen, begging, "Mom?"

She let him flee to his mother. It was better for him to be safely out of the way.

Christine gripped her K2 Meter and flashlight, tools of her trade, descended the stairs one at a time, determined to prove to the latest occupants there was nothing that couldn't be dealt with under the basement stairs — just like her stepfather always insisted — until that night her family fled the home. She had come to finish things left undone. By now, Dr. Christine Mercer, parapsychologist and renowned expert on the paranormal, had seen it all, studied it all, and knew it all. Details of her victorious adulthood were accounted for in her professional resume and the deep lines around her eyes.

Wafts of frigid air blew the smell of mold, pungent laundry detergent, and the dusty stench of those rotting moving boxes into the enclosed decent to the basement. At the bottom? The door. The same untreated, scuffed wood the landlord hung in place after the big flood. Reality matched what crawled out of her memories: the door being a standard, hollow, pressboard door that could easily be kicked in. Or ripped out. Cheap. Why spend on renters?

Her client and son scuffled around the kitchen, just out of sight. His tiny bare feet squeaked on the floor, dragging back remembrances of spilled food, a howling dog, and her stepfather shoving her mother into the wall. He hadn't meant to, he said. It was this house, he said, it made him act crazy. If only they had listened to her.

Hadn't her family moved away? Hadn't that been enough to make things change for the next family?

Only the knick-knacks and throw-away rugs were new. Maybe the photographs on the walls were different. Everything was the same. Except her.

She wasn't frightened *Little Chrissy* anymore. The shoes that tapped on the stairs weren't those patent-leather Mary-Janes that got her mercilessly teased, or that skidded on the sidewalks as she ran home from the park with a bloodied nose. Christine no longer had long braids to clutch protectively so neither the bullies nor the Ghost would yank on them and make her cry. Crying. Always crying. Alone. Outside the house. Inside the house. Nowhere was safe.

The loud thump jarred her from her thoughts. The air was getting colder.

The yellow-metal knob, tarnished over the years, twisted once, squeaking.

Three loud bumps slammed into the walls, echoing in her ears. The boy turned and pressed his face into his mother's stomach. His mother pressed her fingers into his hair and said all the right soothing words.

The scents. The sounds. The familiar growl seeping up from the gap at the base of the door. Christine closed her eyes while mentally subduing Little Chrissy. This was harder than she expected. *Freeze? Run? Hide?*

Little Chrissy had never left her. Damaged children never do. Flashes of the Ghost making her bedroom closet door breathe, or slamming all the windows shut after Mom opened them before going back to work, or the time when all the people in the house were adults and Little Chrissy was sent off to the basement to play — out of sight and mind.

Breathe. Breathe, Christine.

The dirty knob twisted and shook again.

Was a shadow blocking the light from seeping through the gap under the door?

Would the knob be hot too? Her pounding heart climbed steadily to her throat but that too was familiar. The equipment she clutched was the best and latest. *It* was playing with her. Slapping her psyche. Slapping her inner child around. Slapping a child …

Abusing a helpless, neglected child. One who never had a parent around to help when the Ghost crept into her room, frightening her, or when she made her own dinner by herself because they had late meetings or gatherings to go to. Never when she needed them. Never believing her. Not until they were terrified by the Ghost, and their own actions, into fleeing.

How could they have done that to a child? To her?

Christine glanced back up at the boy, who bravely peeked around the corner, and offered him a practiced smile. At least he had his mother. There was so much to be said for that small fact. All Christine could do for him was live up to her reputation.

What she wouldn't have given for —

The light under the door returned.

I'm coming. You and me. We've got history, don't we?

Christine attempted a long, calming breath which only stuttered in her lungs. The bang of her heels overwhelmed the squeaking treads as she deliberately pounded each step down and down to the door, like a countdown for her nemesis.

The knob twisted violently in response. The growl grew louder. The shadow crossed back and forth on the other side. Mustiness and stale odors fell from the shaking doorframe and walls.

Knowing the boy and his mother were listening, she dropped her voice to a whisper. "You abused me. It was you who frightened me back then." Her fingers held out the flashlight like a gun. "Well, I haven't come here to play games. It's time for you to go."

The door almost tore itself off its hinges with uncontrolled shaking, as if screaming, "Bring it on!" at her. Yet it stayed closed.

The dingy yellow knob. It had to be turned. It begged her to turn it.

"You ready to find out what you created in me?" The sides of her mouth rose into a smirk. "You might not like it." She stomped down the last two stairs and onto the linoleum landing, seized the knob, and flung the door open.

Striding into the unaltered basement, the place felt

familiar and foreign at the same time.

Oh hell, some of her toys remained piled near the back where they'd been left behind. The old landlord didn't have the guts to go down there to clean up. Yet … it had been thirty years.

A pair of skates slipped from their resting place. One rolled out to the middle of the floor, pleading to be put on. No longer supported by the skates, a dusty bear lulled over onto its side, eyes still shiny and black. The hours she spent trying to stay upright on those skates, clutching the stuffed bear for comfort and in case she fell. Hours listening to the adults upstairs laughing and talking, while she practiced in hopes of showing them what she'd mastered. Hours of perfecting, with a wary eye on that creepy stairwell.

Grandma's crocheted blanket lay on the floor. Faded garish colors twisted into squares, then linked together in patterns. The warmth it gave her as she would sit in front of the old TV set, watching cartoons until *Soul Train* came on — the universal sign that Saturday morning kid's time was over. Always, the dread of what lurked over her shoulder. But what else could a girl do, all alone on snowy days? Afraid to go out. Afraid to stay in.

Crushed silk flowers pretend boyfriends never gave her. Boxes of puzzles, no doubt with pieces missing. Unopened family games, the wrappers cracking with age. The junk of her youth.

I thought you would never come back. I missed you.

"What?"

We used to play. Then you were gone.

*Do your job.* "You're frightening the family that lives here. You need to stop."

They don't know how to play. Not like you did.

Christine shifted the door, blocking her client from view but not closing off her escape.

Did you tell them you know me?

"You terrified me. Now you're hurting another child. It has to stop."

I played with you. I did tricks for you. Made them show you who they truly were. I watched over you so you would never be alone. We both needed the company so badly.

Warmth, energy, and certainty drained down her arms.

I can do plenty of my old tricks. Growling. Moving things. I've kept in practice.

"No…" her voice was barely above a whisper. "You have to stop."

We've both learned new things. I can show you. You don't need to leave. I am all you need. All you ever needed.

It was there. The Ghost was always there. "Why haven't you moved on?"

I was abandoned. Just like you.

"I'm grown up now."

Are you? Have things changed for you? Are they better?

Christine closed her eyes, tasting the lie as it escaped her lips. "Yes."

And yet, you are still so lonely. But now you've come back home. We can play like we used to, keep each other company like we used to.

The door slammed shut behind her.

# What Burns inside the Sunrise

• • ● • •

## Michael Cooper

## Historical Fiction

Riyadh
January 15, 1902

Abdulaziz Al Saud had come home to find the city gates closed against him. But he would not be denied—not after twelve years in exile.

The young prince crouched in the predawn darkness outside the city wall in whispered consultation with his cousin and one of his brothers. A raiding party of forty fighters clustered around them—the meager force

Abdulaziz had gathered to reclaim the walled city for the House of Saud.

"This is madness!" his cousin whispered out of the darkness. "Raiding the encampments of Bedouin loyal to the Rashidi was one thing, but this is Riyadh! We are a few dozen against hundreds of garrisoned defenders. We have scimitars and a few pistols. They have rifles and a Maxim machine gun!"

"Calm yourself, my cousin. By this time tomorrow, Riyadh will be ours. This was our home and will soon be again!"

"But how can we possibly prevail?" asked his brother in a low voice edged with fear. "We wage war not only against the Rashidi, but also against the Ottomans who support them. Even Father has told us to desist—"

"Do not be troubled, my brother. We have the element of surprise, and once we have taken Riyadh, the Ottomans will switch their support to us. And when our father regains his home and title, he will thank us." He surveyed the raiding party in the half-light. "Spread the word—at first light, we enter the city."

"But surely the sentries will see us—"

"What sentries? We circled the walled city without challenge. It is manifestly clear that the Rashidi are so confident they have not bothered to post sentries. They slumber in the belief that we do not possess the strength or the audacity to attack them. They also believe that they are protected by the city wall—"

"They are—it's twenty feet high!" His cousin's voice, ragged with fear. "How can we *possibly* enter?"

"Have you forgotten how we were able to slip in and out of the city as young boys?" Abdulaziz patted the trunk of a date palm where he knelt by the wall. "This palm bends over the city wall like an elegant siege tower. Here we'll ascend to the battlements of Riyadh." Rising to his feet, he added, "Prepare now for battle!"

As Abdulaziz secured his Colt pistol in the belt of his robe and adjusted the leather sheath of his scimitar, a cold wind blew in from the desert. In the rising wind he heard the dry rustle of the palm fronds, and as the eastern sky began to glow, the sharp edges of the fronds waved like curved scimitars.

In his mind, memories rose—the day Riyadh had fallen to the Rashidi. Even as a boy of fifteen, he had wanted to stay and fight, but his family, the House of Saud, was unprepared and outnumbered. His father insisted they should depart Riyadh and live to fight another day. Aided by the al-Murrah Bedouin, they escaped to the south and found refuge in the Empty Quarter. But summer brought soaring temperatures, burning sand, and deadly scorpions, and they fled again —to Kuwait, where the local ruler, Mubarak Al-Sabah, welcomed them.

In Kuwait, the family settled into a comfortable exile. But not Abdulaziz.

As he grew from boy to man, he also grew in strength

and stature, standing a full head taller than the tallest of his contemporaries. His anger also grew, as did his influence among the young men of the family and beyond. And after twelve years of exile, he'd had enough.

He left Kuwait with a few relatives and friends. Their numbers grew as they raided the encampments of Bedouin loyal to the Rashidi—the tribe that had driven them from Riyadh—the attacks striking fear into their hearts. The Rashidi begged the Ottoman governor to stop the raids. Additional Turkish troops were dispatched.

But Abdulaziz would not be stopped.

In Kuwait, his father heard of the raids and that Abdulaziz planned to attack Riyadh. He sent word— ordering him to stop.

But Abdulaziz would not be stopped.

On the edge of dawn, the wind died, and the palm fronds stopped moving. In the silence Abdulaziz heard the song of a desert lark at the approach of day. Seeing how the russet sky glowed, his heart beat wildly against his ribs, like a caged hawk yearning to fly free.

"What does the Poet ask us?" he whispered to the men pressing in about him. "Who gets up early to discover the moment light begins? Or like Moses, who goes for fire and finds what burns inside the sunrise?" He thrust up a clenched fist. "Who will join me and open the door to another world?"

"We will!" they whispered like the desert wind. "We will!"

Fourteen years later...
*Al-Ahsa Oasis*
Eastern Arabia
April 12, 1916


Standing in the cool shade of a date palm grove, Abdulaziz Al Saud squinted into the afternoon sun as a flag of dust moved toward him. Major General Sir Percy Cox, the Chief Colonial Officer of British India, was coming to counsel, and Abdulaziz knew why.

Sir Percy was based in Basra, and through a flurry of messages, they had decided to meet at the oasis instead of in Riyadh, shortening Sir Percy's journey by two hundred miles.

Abdulaziz watched the Rolls-Royce motorcar come into view, and it soon rattled to a stop within a stone's throw of where he stood.

The rear door opened, and Percy stepped out, raising his hand in greeting. "How very good to see you again, *ya Abdulaziz!*" he exclaimed in perfect Najdi Arabic, "How is my favorite Arab tribal leader and statesman?"

"Excellent well, thank you, Sir Percy, but *Arab tribal*

*leader and statesman?* Couldn't you simply call me, Your Excellency?" Laughing, Abdulaziz extended his hand, "*Salaam alaykum!*"

"*W'alaykum as salaam,* Your Excellency!"

"How was your journey from Basra?"

"Long and hot." Cox sighed, took off his helmet, and wiped perspiration from his forehead. "I am most looking forward to spirited conversations and besting you at chess, Your Excellency."

Abdulaziz nodded his assent to Cox. The tall Englishman was close to his own height, thin and distinguished looking with wavy silver hair. As befitting a British military attaché, he was arrayed in a gray officer's uniform, with matching helmet, shirt, and tie.

"I am grateful to you for suggesting we meet here instead of Riyadh, Sire." Cox continued. "Not only did it shorten my journey, but I have long wanted to see this verdant corner of your realm."

"I was more than happy to accommodate you, my friend. Even so, you traveled far—five hundred miles from Basra. When did you depart?"

"Long before dawn this morning, Sire. Hard to believe it's been only three months since we met in Darin." Percy looked to the east. "How far is that from here?"

"A hundred miles that way." Abdulaziz pointed. "On the Arabian Gulf coast."

Percy smiled. "Don't you mean, the *Persian* Gulf

coast, Sire?"

"Let the Persians call it what they will—for me it is the *Arabian* Gulf!" Laughing, he turned to Percy. "Allow me to offer you and your driver some refreshment after your long journey. Please." He nodded toward a black goatskin tent pitched among the date palms, and turning, led the way into the tent, where he commanded a servant, "Bring cool water and dates for our guests."

Turning to Cox, he said, "I will have my men raise a similar tent for you and your driver—with sitting room, bedrooms, and water closet—so you may be comfortable during your time here. Until then, you are most welcome to use all the amenities I have. We have already slaughtered a young lamb, and in a few hours, we'll dine together."

The servant returned with a tray.

"Please, refresh yourselves!" As they ate and drank, he asked Percy, "Shall I have soap, hot water and towels provided for your bath?"

Cox smiled and spat a date pit into his closed hand. "That would be grand, Sire! How very generous of you —"

"Don't mention it! I'm merely fulfilling the clause in the Treaty of Darin providing for your bathing!"

Percy's eyes narrowed. "I don't remember anything about bathing, Your Excellency, but I well remember the terms of the treaty."

Hearing a change in Percy's tone of voice, Abdulaziz

nodded toward the tent flap opening. "Might we have a word while I give you a short tour of the palm grove?" He led the way to a stream along a path bordered by lush grass and flowering oleander. "So, Sir Percy, it appears we are to revisit the Treaty of Darin."

"Yes, Your Excellency. That is why I'm here."

"Very well." Though Abdulaziz generally didn't trust the British, in a strange way, he trusted Percy Cox, considering him the best of a bad lot. "Please, speak that I may know your mind."

"I am sure you recall that the treaty obligated Great Britain to safeguard your territory, which we have done by making the lands of the House of Saud a British protectorate. We have also acknowledged the right of your sons to rule after you. The treaty also obligates Great Britain to define your borders as well as guaranteeing the sovereignty of the smaller regional British Protectorates—the sheikhdoms of Kuwait, Qatar, Dubai, Abu Dhabi, and a few others. You no doubt also recall that the treaty obligated us to provide you with weapons, ammunition and twenty thousand pounds sterling to defend your lands. All this we have done. Additionally, I am certain you recall that the treaty obligated us to provide you with a monthly stipend of five thousand gold sovereigns—"

"Also, this you have done, Sir Percy, and I am most grateful!" As Abdulaziz saw Sir Percy nod in acknowledgment, he noticed that he didn't seem particularly happy as he continued speaking.

"In return, the treaty called for you to make war against your mortal enemy, Ibn Rashid since he is allied with the Ottomans—"

"This I have done!" Abdulaziz cut in. "I have attacked the House of Rashid in Ha'il and throughout the Nejd without pause!" But even as he spoke, the words sounded hollow.

Percy raised his shoulders. "Fighting with Ibn Rashid is something you do as naturally as you breathe—with or without our urging! We both know that the House of Saud has battled the Rashidi for centuries. That is not the issue at hand."

Abdulaziz frowned as Percy continued.

"Sire, you agreed to enter the war against the Ottoman Empire as an ally of Great Britain."

For a long moment, Abdulaziz said nothing. He looked out over the stream, past the perfect white oleander flowers toward a stand of date palms. When he spoke, his voice was a whisper. "*That* is the clause of the treaty which poses for us a great challenge…"

"Why is that?"

Abdulaziz fixed Percy with his eyes. "Because, my friend, it appears likely that Great Britain will lose this war, and if we are allied with you, the Turks will destroy the House of Saud."

## British-occupied Basra
## Iraq

Slightly lifting the hem of her silk gown, Gertrude Bell descended the winding staircase in the palatial home Sir Percy and Lady Cox were renting during their extended sojourn in Basra. As their houseguest for the past week, this was to be Gertrude's first formal dinner and she was looking forward to it. Though saddened by the absence of Sir Percy, Gertrude was delighted that they would be joined by her colleague from the Cairo Arab Bureau, Colonel Thomas Edward Lawrence, or Ned as he was known to his friends.

Upon entering the parlor, Gertrude saw Lady Cox, attired in a purple chiffon gown with lightly padded shoulders, arranging roses in a lavender vase.

"Good evening, Lady Cox. I must say, your roses are gorgeous!"

"Thank you, my dear, but no credit to me. They thrive in warm climates. After all, this Eden is where roses originated."

"When did Sir Percy leave for Arabia?"

"Very early this morning, my dear. I'm so very sorry he was called away." She shrugged, raising her padded shoulders. "However, the imperatives of wartime require immediate action."

Gertrude nodded. "He told me as much yesterday, and I quite concur—especially since Ibn Saud may be key to our fortunes in Arabia against the Ottomans." She glanced at the salon door and asked, "Has Lawrence arrived from Cairo?"

"Yes, he has, my dear. He's freshening up and will be joining us soon. While we wait, would you care for an aperitif?" She picked up a crystal bell and rang. "A Pimm's cup, perhaps?"

"That would be lovely."

After conveying her request to a servant, Lady Cox turned back to Gertrude. "I'm so looking forward to speaking with Colonel Lawrence. Have you known him long?"

"Oh, yes. We collaborated years ago on a few digs in Mesopotamia. Nowadays, we're working together at the Arab Bureau in Cairo, doing all we can to leverage British influence in the Levant."

"Sir Percy does the same here in Mesopotamia, and fervently believes that alliances with local leaders will tip the scales in our favor on the Middle East Front, which he believes is crucial for victory the Great War."

"I couldn't agree more, Lady Cox. His insight into diplomatic subtleties in the region is remarkable." Gertrude had long admired Percy Cox. A shrewd and honest man, so unlike many of the British diplomats maneuvering between the British Raj, Persia, and the Gulf protectorates.

"Percy speaks to me endlessly about it all. He also mentioned that you have recently visited Delhi—to sort out things between British Egypt and British India—feuding at a time when they should be cooperating." She smiled and added, "Percy attributes it to strong-willed men competing with each other, and believes they've managed to tie themselves into one very large Gordian Knot!"

"An apt metaphor, Lady Cox. Sir Percy certainly has a way with words."

"You'll be happy to know that Percy believes that you are the person best able to deal with these squabbling men and to untie the knot."

"But the knot has grown so, it's nigh impossible to untie." Gertrude sighed. "Sadly, and unlike Alexander, I cannot simply dispose of it with a sharp sword."

"You have a sharp mind, my dear, and know the Levant better than any European. That makes you the natural choice to smooth over these fractious relations between our people in India and in Egypt. Especially since you know how to deal with strong-willed men!"

Gertrude smiled. "Such as Lawrence."

"Is Colonel Lawrence a strong-willed fellow?"

"Decidedly so, though you wouldn't know it to see him. He's quite diminutive—almost a foot shorter than Sir Percy. He's also very shy and just twenty-eight years old. But he's relentlessly brilliant and has a will of iron."

"How very intriguing! Will he be staying long in Basra?"

"Sadly, no. Tomorrow he travels to Kut al-Amara to

meet secretly with Ottoman military authorities to convince them to lift the siege of the British-Indian force marooned there." She leaned toward Lady Cox and added in a low voice, "I have it on good authority that Lawrence is bringing two million pounds sterling to give the Turks in exchange for our troops, though it's very hush-hush—if that became widely known, he probably wouldn't reach Kut alive."

"If only he succeeds!" Lady Cox sighed. "Those boys have been surrounded there for months!"

A servant entered the parlor with their Pimm's cups. As Gertrude studied the glass in her hand, feeling the coolness of it, she felt a stab of guilt. *Here I am, surrounded by luxury with a mint sprig and orange slice suspended in my drink while our soldiers are trapped and dying two hundred miles away.* As she took a sip, she saw Lawrence enter the parlor.

"Sorry to be tardy, Lady Cox," he said with a bow. "I hope you ladies haven't already finished dinner…"

"We wouldn't dream of starting without you!" She raised her glass and directed a servant, "One for the gentleman, please."

Accustomed to seeing Lawrence disheveled and in baggy clothing, Gertrude was pleasantly surprised to see him very appropriately attired for the occasion; his crisp uniform replete with Sam-Browne belt, and the mop of blond hair atop his high forehead parted and brushed smartly to the side. He fixed Gertrude with his gentian blue eyes, and she detected his discomfiture at being so presentable.

Lady Cox offered her hand. "How was your trip, Colonel Lawrence?"

"Delightful, since it's led me here, Lady Cox." With a low bow he grazed her glove with his lips, straightened up, and said with a little smile, "After rocking on the currents of the Red Sea and Persian Gulf for the past week, I'm looking forward to a dining experience that doesn't move."

"And you shall have it, along with excellent cuisine!"

As Lawrence approached Gertrude, she extended her gloved hand and managed not to laugh at his dutiful adherence to a formal ritual she knew he detested.

"Miss Bell," he said with a bow.

"Good to see you, Ned, but I'm certain that you're as disappointed as I that Sir Percy isn't able to join us."

"We all have our duties, Miss Bell, and speaking of which, how was Delhi?"

"I made definite progress in reconciling our squabbling administrations. I was just speaking with Lady Cox about the fact that British India and British Egypt too often work at cross-purposes, and often with calamitous results."

"It's precisely one of those catastrophes I'm to address in Kut, and once I return here, I look forward to hearing all about your talks in Delhi—all the better to communicate that information to Cairo—"

"But, Ned," Gertrude cut in, confused, "I'm perfectly capable of speaking for myself when I return to Cairo."

Lawrence seemed to hesitate a moment before he replied. "I'm afraid you won't be returning to Cairo, Gertrude. Not for a while, anyway."

"Sorry?" she asked, taken aback. "I'm to remain in Basra?"

"For the coming year or so. The bureau is quite impressed by your ability to coordinate policy in Mesopotamia and Arabia. They feel you're indispensable." Lawrence shrugged. "I should think you'd be pleased…"

"I am, Ned," Gertrude smiled as she quickly regained her composure. "I'm delighted to contribute to the war effort in any way I can."

"You're more than welcome to stay here with us, Gertrude," said Lady Cox as a servant entered with a Pimm's cup for Lawrence.

He took the glass and raised it. "Ladies, to your very good health! As the Bard wrote in the Merry Wives; let us drink down all unkindness!"

"Dinner is served," intoned a servant.

Lady Cox was soon seated at the head of the table with Gertrude and Lawrence to her left and right.

Now reconciled to her posting in Basra, Gertrude drew a deep breath as wine was poured into cut crystal glasses beside neatly folded white napkins and shining cutlery. A white linen tablecloth glowed beneath the soft rays of a candelabra hung with crystal prisms. It was all beautiful, but her heart was heavy as her thoughts returned to the marooned British troops. She shook the thoughts away as Lady Cox turned to Lawrence.

"Percy so wanted to meet you, Colonel, but he had an urgent meeting with Abdulaziz. Though I've never met the man, Percy tells me he's quite impressive."

"Quite so!" said Gertrude. "He's a giant of a man with a commanding presence and strikingly handsome. Small wonder men follow him, and women are drawn to him. What's more," she raised her eyebrows, "By my last count, he has thirty-one wives!"

"How simply scandalous!" gasped Lady Cox.

"Sounds simply exhausting," said Lawrence.

Seeing Lady Cox blush, Gertrude hastened to redirect the conversation. "I believe he is the ideal Arab Sheik to lead the revolt against the Turks."

"That opinion is not widely shared," said Lawrence. "Those of us in Cairo are counting on Prince Faisal of the Hashemites."

"Why the disagreement?" asked Lady Cox.

"Simply put," said Gertrude with barely concealed indignation, "Colonel

Lawrence and the others in Cairo have never actually met Abdulaziz. I have, and believe he would be the better choice."

Lady Cox shook her head. "I fear Percy might not agree with you, my dear."

Not expecting to be contradicted, Gertrude was flustered. "But, my dear Lady Cox, didn't you just tell us how impressive Sir Percy thought him to be?"

"Yes, but it appears that Abdulaziz is somewhat hesitant to support Great Britain in the war, which is precisely why Sir Percy isn't here with us now. He's gone to speak with Abdulaziz about honoring the Treaty of Darin, which among other things requires him to ally with Great Britain."

"I can understand his reluctance," said Lawrence with a sigh. "After the disasters of Gallipoli and Kut, I'd be surprised if anyone could convince Abdulaziz to support us. He undoubtedly believes that he has nothing to gain and everything to lose. Prince Faisal, however, welcomes the challenge."

Gertrude bit back a sharp retort as a servant entered pushing a cart with an ornate soup tureen. After serving soup with bread roll and butter to each diner, the servant withdrew and Gertrude spoke up.

"But, Ned, Abdulaziz is doing all he can. Have you forgotten how he has clashed with Ibn Rashid? How he wrested the Al-Ahsa Oasis away from the Ottomans?" Gertrude wasn't done scolding Lawrence, but when she heard Lady Cox clear her throat, she realized that she had raised her voice. Lawrence had that effect on her.

"That was rude of me, Ned. I'm sorry."

"No, Gertrude. It is I who should apologize—casting a pall on this lovely evening with my Arabian musings…"

"You have a valid point, Ned," Gertrude said as she buttered a roll. "Abdulaziz *is* hesitant. He's concerned about his fortunes should he ally with us. I wish there was some way of convincing him that by fighting on our side, he could turn the tide in our favor. I wish I knew the words that might convince him, but I have no idea what they might be."

Lady Cox reached out and placed her hand on Gertrude's. "As we speak, my dear, I know that Percy is searching for those very words."

● ● ● ●

*Al-Ahsa Oasis*
Eastern Arabia

Reclining after dinner, Abdulaziz sipped coffee with Sir Percy in the fragrant half-light of the tent lit by a single lantern and warmed by coals glowing in the open hearth. Though his blunt remarks to Percy seemed to hang like a heavy partition between them, he was glad that he had spoken honestly. He indeed hoped Percy might find a way to assuage his concerns. Truly, the dangers of allying with a weakened British Empire were genuine, and the consequences ruinous for the House of Saud in alliance with a defeated England.

*But I do feel a natural affection for this Englishman,* he thought, *and my relations with the Ottomans have always been strained.*

Abdulaziz sighed and took another sip of coffee. *And it's also true that I signed a treaty with Great Britain, and we broke bread to bind our friendship, and shared salt as a promise of that bond.*

An ember in the dying fire snapped, and in the silence that followed, Abdulaziz heard Sir Percy speak, his voice calm, his words measured.

"To what may the thing be likened, Your Excellency? The date palms flourish in this oasis because of the unhurried seepage of a hidden aquifer through hundreds of springs. So, too, does the reservoir of our friendship support a fertile future." Percy leaned forward and whispered, "Speak to me further of your concerns, my friend."

"I will. Given that you British are bogged down in France, routed at Gallipoli, and defeated at Kut, why should I cast my lot with you? Can one mold the desert sand into shape? Why would I alienate the Turks with whom I will have to live when this war is over? Why would I risk the very existence of the House of Saud and the lives of my children? I could very well end up on the wrong side of history." He left off speaking and finished his coffee, tasting the bitterness of the grounds at the bottom of the cup.

"You have posed good questions, Your Excellency, and much of what you have said is true. But you are ignoring the pivotal role you might play in affecting the outcome of the war. When you speak about the right or wrong side of history, consider which outcome is truly right and which is wrong. All the excellent questions you pose can be distilled down to a single question—why is it vital for the future of your people that you ally with the British?"

"Indeed, why?"

"My answer to you is two words—Kaiser Wilhelm."

"What manner of answer is that? The Kaiser is of no concern to me or my house."

"Please hear me out, Your Excellency. Is it not inscribed in the Quran? *Those who have faith in the Quran and those who follow the Jewish faith, and the Christians, indeed, all who believe in God and do righteous deeds, shall not fear nor grieve.*"

"What is your meaning?"

"Just this, Sire. Outwardly, Germany appears to be a Christian nation, with its many Catholics and Lutherans. But beneath the surface for the last thirty, there has been a revival of the old German Paganism with worship of the old Norse gods." Percy paused and drew a deep breath. "I am sad to say that Germany is now, at its heart, no longer a Christian nation."

"What are you saying? Of course it is."

Percy shook his head. "Many Germans have turned away from the true God of Abraham, turning even from God's prophet, Jesus. Following the Kaiser's example, they turn to pagan German gods."

"Preposterous!" Abdulaziz shot back. "The Kaiser not a Christian? Impossible! And what possible *advantage* is there for him to turn to pagan gods?"

"It isn't about advantage, Your Excellency. It's what the Kaiser has come to believe. Moreover, he views Arabs, Jews, Africans and all non-Germanic or Nordic races as inferior. His faith is based on the supremacy of the German people under the protection of pagan German gods."

"But how can this be? He made a Christian pilgrimage to the Holy Land and had himself crowned King of Jerusalem!"

"That is only because he seeks the power and the name of Jerusalem. In truth, Kaiser Wilhelm wishes to reign from a pagan palace he will build within the sacred precincts upon the Holy Mountain—in the very place where the Mosque of Omar now stands!"

"Nonsense! The Turks will never allow it."

"The Turks?" Cox exhaled a quick laugh. "The Kaiser despises the Turks just as he despises the Arabs, Jews, Armenians, and all non-Nordic people. He considers them all inferior. And when he rules a German empire from the Rhine to the Euphrates, the Turks, who are now his puppets, will be his vassals, and you will be his slaves."

Cox's words struck deep into the heart of Abdulaziz. For a long minute he kept his own counsel. *I have heard rumors of the Kaiser's disdain for Muslims even as he claimed to have converted to Islam, which everyone knows is a sham. While I have always considered this a harmless deception, there is nothing harmless about what Percy has said about the Kaiser's true goals. I have witnessed the* construction *of the Berlin to Baghdad railway with plans to extend the rails to Basra and Mecca—traversing Arabia with an envenomed and ensnaring spider web!*

Turning to Percy, he said. "Your words have been illuminating, my friend. You have obliged me to reconsider my decision, however, I remain concerned. The Germans are so formidable in battle, and the Turkish armies so vast. Can they truly be stopped?"

"They can, Your Excellency, and with your support, they will! Consider that the British Empire rules India and Egypt, and is also master of the seas, just as the Arabs are masters of the desert. Germany and Turkey will grow weak as they face the combined might of England together with her French and Russian allies, and all the nations of the British Empire—Australia, Ireland, New Zealand, India, Canada, and perhaps soon, her former colony of the United States. With such an alliance, along with the crucial contribution of the Arabs, the combined force against Germany and the Turks in the Levant will be as an iron wall. The Central Powers will shatter against it!"

Abdulaziz rose from the carpet, his heart racing—not with fear, but with joy. *I recall this same feeling of exultation when I crouched with my men outside the walls of Riyadh. Now as then, I stand at a turning point—at the threshold of a new world. Now as then, it is I, Abdulaziz al Saud, who controls my fate! Then I chose to fix my gaze upon that which could be gained, not what might be lost. Now I shall do the same!*

He rose to his full height. "Sir Percy, I will join you in this war! I am certain that the unholy alliance of the Ottoman Empire and their German conspirators will vanish like a cloud chased by a storm! It is as the Poet has written; 'Begin walking toward shams! Your legs will get heavy and tired. Then comes a moment of feeling the wings you have grown, lifting!'"

# The Voice

## J.W. Bell

## Paranormal

I know. I don't have the money to buy a book. I don't have any money at all. Never do. It sucks, but it's true. I'm here because I followed that nebulous feeling that told me to go in. It's crazy. There is this voice …

*Again, with the nebulous things?*

Is life just a collection of vague experiences that I react to? It's getting to be just that, and I'm not sure how I got here. Uh, this way … became like this.

My eyes were hungry and devoured the room full of books, catching glimpses of titles that intrigued me, *The Razor's Edge*, *Siddhartha*, and even *The Fountainhead*. The store has great books here.

I would've known this place was a bookstore, even with my eyes closed. The delicious smell of them. The aroma of libraries and bookstores, with the sharp bite of the newly printed. Hell, this smell is better than the scent of a new car. When I went to school, I spent whole classes with my nose jabbed into a new book to sniff it. Yeah, teachers probably thought me reading, devouring the wisdom inside, but no, I was content to be an actual moron stuck in an olfactory orgy.

Besides, the voice said …

Oh, and don't let me forget the dust. There is always dust in bookstores or libraries, too.

"Listen, Bubba. You need to go."

I snapped around to see the asshole running this place with his neatly combed hair, shirt, and tie. My arms shot up to keep him away. "I'm not doing anything wrong!" He could maybe hurt me with his flailing around like that. "Come on, man. I'm not harming anything. I just want to read a little."

"Out, Bubba. We both know you aren't here to read. You're here to beg my customers for mone–"

"No, man. I like it here. The books–"

"Out!"

I walked toward the door and pulled the book up for one last sniff, but the prick snatched it away and pushed me in the direction I was going in the first place. My foot caught on something, and I launched forward, flailing around to find something to grab as I flew, but there was just air, and the woman.

"Hey!" Her voice carried both surprise and anger as she fell backward to the glass door, then down.

The next thing I knew, all kinds of shit crashed onto the floor, a few things broke, and I thumped to the ground and on top of the woman's legs. I tried to apologize with my eyes. But she was busy. Her eyes scolded me, and then she turned them away and tried to burn a hole through the prick of a bookstore manager.

I clambered to my feet and held out my hand to help her. She grasped it and pulled herself up, still trying to melt the asshole. Then she turned to me and gasped, dropping my hand. She moved away like I was Typhoid Mary.

The woman was pretty in an odd sort of way. Her hair was the color of the mouse I saw this morning, brownish gray. Her eyes were blue and would appear deep with hidden secrets if she wasn't so aggressively pissed. Anyway, her hair stuck out everywhere, like all those women trying to pretend they weren't losing their hair, thinning away.

I wondered if she was why the voice told me to come in here. It does that kind of shit. I will ask it later.

As I pushed the door open and strolled out, the sun hit my eyes and made me squint, so I put my hand up to shield them.

"Get away from me!" The woman again. I guess she got tired of trying to blister the bookstore manager.

I backed away from her. "What?"

"Get away! You tried to hit me. I saw you raising your arm to strike."

This lady is loony. "Lady, you're crazy."

The voice told me to back up and let the sun strike me in the eyes, which I did. And be damned, she stopped squawking. Now she stared.

"Can I help you, lady?"

She made a horrifying face like she was standing off stage when Medea killed her kids. "You poor man."

I looked around to see who she was talking to. Nobody but me on the street.

"What can I help you with, lady?" She confused the hell out of me. Maybe the voice understood. She was as confused as a woodpecker with rubber lips and driven mad by an unbelievable world. Dunno, except I knew she had something wrong.

She straightened herself like dignity folded around her, then she donned an air of superiority like the sweater she wore and looked down on me, even though I was taller by a couple of inches. Her eyes became deep like I knew they could, and she rubbernecked around to see if anyone would see her talking to me. It must've been alright because she held her hand out to me, not to shake or even place it on my shoulder. It was more like she invited me to follow her.

The voice urged me to go. So, I nodded and walked toward the lady. She turned, still holding her arm out behind her, and walked. The warmth of the sun felt wonderful on my back.

"My name is Beverly. Beverly Yorkshire." Her voice

was the kind that makes me feel like she cared, not real high or low, but fuzzy.

I grunted in acknowledgment.

"Can I know your name?"

"Sure. It's–"

No. It doesn't matter.

That was strange. But I shut up.

"Don't want to tell me? I promise I won't tell anyone." She stopped talking for a couple of steps. "Hmm. How about I call you George? My husband was named George. He's no longer around. Is that alright if I call you George?"

"But my name isn't George."

"I can't just call you, uh. I believe the bookstore man called you Bubba—"

"Yes, Bubba." That should work. I still didn't give my name like the voice said not to.

"Are you sure? Bubba?"

I nodded a couple of times. "Yes, call me Bubba." We walked by an alley, and I smelled ripe garbage from the Chinese place's dumpster. Beverly smelled it too. She scrunched her face and took her finger across her nose. It didn't bother me like that, though.

Today was Wednesday, so there wouldn't be anything good to eat there. The garbage truck came by here on Wednesday afternoon. Today was the best day for pizza. Yesterday was their pick-up day, and last night they had their buffet. I'll check it later.

*Follow Beverly.*

Okay. I won't lose her. She's walking kind of slowly.

*She needs help.*

I figured. Otherwise, you wouldn't tell me about the woman.

Beverly stopped in front of the door to the diner. "Can I get you something to eat? Uh, Bubba?"

I made a mistake when I looked at her eyes again. I fell into them. The blueness sucked me right in, and I grabbed the door frame. It was hard to keep from falling because they made me unbalanced.

How come she needs my help?

*Because she does.*

But—

*She does.*

Okay, okay.

"Bubba? Are you hungry?" She held the door open.

I peered inside. That bastard would kick me out. This place is where the old man with a bat is, and I hunched my back and furiously blinked while I weighed the problem. There was the Pizza feast, but the chunks of hamburgers they had here were good— but that shitty bat. I decided on pizza and opened my mouth to tell her.

*No.*

Her eyes grabbed me again. Between the sight of them, and the voice, I nodded and stepped into the place.

"Hey!"

Shit. It was the baseball bat bastard.

Be damned! Beverly jumped in front of me, and the guy stopped and settled on pounding his hand, of course not as hard as he pounds on me.

Beverly scolded the man with her eyes and turned to look at me with, I suppose, sympathy, but it turned out she put the sweater of superiority back on. Her eyeball conversation was, "Leave him alone!" Then she turned to me. "You poor bastard, Bubba."

The bat guy walked back behind the counter to put his bat up and pointed at me.

"We'll sit here," Beverly indicated a booth out of the way but near the door. "Come on, Bubba."

I sat, trying to look in every direction I could.

"It's alright. No one will harm you."

I nodded. "Thank you."

*Tell her.*

?

*Tell her. Telling her is why you are here. Say, she's okay.*

Oh. I nodded several times.

"Now, what would you like to eat, Bubba?" She picked up the menu from where it sat, wedged behind the napkin holder. "Bubba, you can have anything. I'll buy whatever you want."

The woman talking was a new Beverly for me. Hell, she sounded chipper, like a rabbit enjoying the funny carrot farm. She didn't even look over her shoulder.

I pointed to the double cheeseburger with tomatoes, lettuce, and pickles, all on top of a mountain of fried potatoes. My mouth was anticipating, and my tongue was wandering around my mouth.

"We'll have the deluxe cheeseburger, please."

*Tell her.*

Can't I wait until I eat?

*Now.*

I won't get the burger, though.

*Tell. Her. Now.*

Shit. "Miss Beverly?"

"Why yes, Bubba. Do you need something else?"

I shook my head. "No, mam. I just need to tell you she's okay."

Her eyes pulled her head around, and she stared wide-eyed.

I fell into them again and had to scramble to hang onto the table so I wouldn't drown there. My hands and arms hurt from how hard I grabbed the table.

Her fuzzy voice was gone, replaced with an edgy one. "What are you talking about?" I thought the edgy sound was going to cut my ears. And her eyes wouldn't let go, either.

I pushed backward to escape, blinking several times to stop staring at her. It didn't work. They stared at me so hard! I thought her soul was fighting to snatch mine.

*It's Fine.*

"Hell no, it isn't! Why did you want me to—"

"Bubba, who are you talking about?"

I looked for a way out, but there wasn't any. There was only the room – as blue as her eyes. Damn. Damn!

The voice called to me, but I tried to shake it off.

The blue eyes were pissed, hard as ice. "Who? Bubba, Who?" Her shrill voice pierced me. She grabbed my shoulders, and I couldn't move. The eyes hurt me, so I turned my head. I wanted to melt away, but my eyes wouldn't let go.

I couldn't. Damn.

*Her daughter.*

Tell her that?

Beverly relaxed her grip on me and stopped screaming. Her eyes blinked like a spinster at a wedding. They welled up and tears dripped down her cheeks. "Who, Bubba?"

*Now.*

"Your daughter." I hung my head, resting it on my chest. Someone put the burger on the table in front of me. My nose filled with the aroma—it was fresh food. I stared at it, while my hand sneaked to it and seized it.

"Bubba, do you know my daughter?"

I took a huge bite and chewed. My head shook. "No." I chewed as fast as I could. Then I jammed it into the side of my mouth. "I don't know you or her. I just know she's fine."

"Are you sure? Do you know my daughter's name? Because, if you do, I could believe you. I desperately want to believe you, but … How did you know I even had a daughter?"

"The voice." I'd forgotten how delicious food is without the taint in it. The flavors burst through my mouth—another bite.

My arms trembled, and I bounced around like a kid needing to pee.

Beverly sat as still as death. She breathed in and sighed. "Bubba, do you hear voices?"

I closed my eyes so I wouldn't fall into her eyes again. My head shook. "No. I just hear one, sometimes, but not always."

Her shoulders sagged. "Does it tell you to do things?"

"Yes. But not always."

"Does it tell you to hurt people?"

I stuck the last burger piece in my mouth so they couldn't kick me out before I could eat it.

"I don't hurt anyone." My eyes flicked around to see where everybody was. The door looked close, but I'd have to go around the other table.

Beverly was doing the same thing. Her eyes flew everywhere. Then her arm flailed some, and the bastard with the baseball bat came to the table, the bat behind his back.

That bastard stared at me as he talked. "Can I help you, mam?"

"Yes, I wondered if you would be so kind as to help me?" The blue things dragged across me, and then they focused on him. "I don't think I have an urgent need or anything. I'm simply inquiring as to availability."

I knew what she was saying. She thought I might turn dangerous. She thinks, oh, the eyes turned on me. They are going to hurt me. I kept my eyes lowered so I wouldn't fall into the blue.

Why did I have to tell her?

*Because she needs to know before …*

Now it was my turn to be a statue. Before what?

"Okay, Bub. Time for you to go." The baseball bat man stood before us, the bat now in front of him, his head pointing to the door.

I scooched to where I could stand up. My eyes looked at the table. The fries would be gone, and I was careful not to look Beverly in the eyes.

*Tell her, Tina. Just tell her, Tina.*

I leaned down toward Beverly. "Her name is Tina."

Beverly sucked in sharply.

Before I could stand all the way, Beverly screamed. "That's it!" The blue eyes swallowed me.

Then, the bat hit me in the neck.

"Oh, my God, Suzie!" Tina waved her friend over, backed the video up, and pointed to the picture. "Look at this. My mother is going viral."

"In the video?"

"Says … homeless man was attacking Mrs. Beverly

Yorkshire when Gary Owen, owner of the Grand Avenue Diner, saved her. The unidentified man is in critical condition at the hospital and under suspicion of murdering Mrs. Yorkshire's daughter, Tina, who has been missing now for three months. The man, believed to have mental problems, will undergo psychiatric care at …'"

"Holy shit, Tina. They think you're dead."

"Yeah, maybe I better go on back home." Tina started to gather her things and start packing.

"What are you doing?"

Tina turned. "I'm getting ready to go home, of course."

Suzie leaned back and put her feet on the coffee table. "Why? We can take our time. It won't matter at all when we get there. Even if they find him guilty of your murder, he'll just go to some funny farm. They said he's crazy."

Tina blinked and stared at her best friend.

# About the Authors

## D. Krauss

D. Krauss resides in the Shenandoah Valley, Virginia. He has been a cottonpicker, a sodbuster, a librarian, a surgical orderly, the guy who paints the little white line down the middle of the road, a weatherman, a door-kickin' shove-gun-in-face lawman, an analyst, and a school bus driver. Currently, he's a layabout. He's married and has a wildman bass guitarist for a son.

## Donald Firesmith

Donald Firesmith is a multi-award-winning author of speculative fiction, including science fiction, fantasy, paranormal horror, and modern urban paranormal novels and collections of short stories. Because of his strong background in software/system engineering and science, his science fiction is well-researched, and he relies on numerous science, technology, and military-technical advisors to ensure that the non-speculative aspects of his stories are realistic and believable. He lives in Pittsburgh, Pennsylvania, with his wife Becky, and varying numbers of dogs and cats.

## Lisa Reifsnider

Lisa Reifsnider turned to writing when her youngest went off to college forcing her into retirement. After taking several classes and participating in a few National Writing Months, she found her stride. She has written several short stories and is close to completing her first novel. She lives outside Brussels, Belgium with her husband of over 30 years, Jason and their grumpy old dachshund, Dagwood.

## Michael Deeze

Michael Deeze is a natural-born storyteller—in life and in print. A child of the sixties, he draws extensively from his own diverse experiences and subsequent education to introduce the hapless Emmett Casey. As U.S. Army veteran and retired Doctor of Chiropractic, Deeze now lives in Illinois after spending decades living near the forests of northern Wisconsin. He's a devoted father to his three children, a magical daughter, two grown sons, and his dog. His first novels are the critically acclaimed Bless Me Father, and For I have Sinned, The Heretic is the final novel in the series.

## David Hagerty

David Hagerty is the author of the Duncan Cochrane mystery series, which chronicles crime and dirty politics in his hometown of Chicago. Real events inspired all four novels, including the murder of a politician's daughter six weeks before election day (They Tell Me

You Are Wicked), a series of sniper killings in the city's most notorious housing project (They Tell Me You Are Crooked), and the Tylenol poisonings (They Tell Me You Are Brutal). He has also published more than 50 short stories online and in print.

## T. E. MacArthur

T. E. MacArthur, author, artist, historian, amateur cat whisperer, and parapsychologist wannabe living in the San Francisco Bay Area. She wrote the standout Steampunk series, The Volcano Lady, and the Gaslight Adventures of Tom Turner. A Place of Fog and Murder is her Noir-punk mystery, bringing a fantasy sci-fi 1930s San Francisco to life with her tough-as-nails femme-fatale-detective, Lou Tanner P.I., through exciting car chases and Chandleresque witty repartee. She's even written for several local and specialized publications, anthologies, and was an accidental sports reporter for Reuters News.

## Michael J Cooper

Michael J Cooper writes historical fiction set at major turning points in the Middle East; Foxes in the Vineyard, set in 1948 won the 2011 Indie Publishing Contest grand prize, The Rabbi's Knight, set in 1290 was a finalist for the 2014 CIBA Chaucer Award for historical fiction, and Wages of Empire set at the start of WW1 won the CIBA 2022 grand prize for young adult fiction and the Hemingway first prize for wartime historical fiction. A native of Berkeley, California, Cooper emigrated to Israel in 1966, studying and working there for the next decade; he lived in Jerusalem during the last year the city was divided between Israel and Jordan and graduated from Tel Aviv University Medical School. Now a pediatric cardiologist in Northern California, he travels to the region twice a year on volunteer missions for Palestinian children who lack access to care.

## J.W. Bell

J.W. Bell's life reads like an adventure story. He was a Field Artillery Officer in the Army for ten years, is well-versed in long-range and large-caliber weapons, and is an expert with small arms — oh yes, he trained in explosives and is excellent with hand grenades. His military thrillers use actual terminology, weapons, and military courtesy. He traveled extensively throughout Europe, Asia, and the U.S., living in Hawaii for several years. He coached gymnastics for a time and worked for years as a roughneck in the oilfields of Oklahoma. He became a teacher and holds a lifetime teaching license to teach music and drama. He composed his first symphony and now has a good start on his second. He is the author of *The Sigma Code Chronicles*, and recently branched out into metaphysics with *I Am, Therefore I Think*.

Thank you for taking the time to read this collection fromIndies United Publishing House. We hope you enjoyed it and would like to encourage you to take a moment to review this collection on your favorite reading platform.

## A little about Indies United

Here at Indies United, we are a co-op of like-minded authors working together to showcase our books and highlight our diversity as writers. We openly encourage and support both new and established authors in their pursuit of finding their audience while bringing to you books worth reading. Our goal is to give authors a home to call their own, while bringing fresh, innovative, and exciting books to readers all over the world.

If you are an author, please check us out at www.indiesunited.net